PLAGUE OF THE DREAMLESS

Published in Canada by Engen Books, St. John's, NL.

ISBN-13: 978-1-989473-91-7

Distributed by:
Engen Books
www.engenbooks.com
submissions@engenbooks.com

First mass market paperback printing: November 2020

Cover Design: Ellen Curtis

Slipstreamers Committee:
Amanda Labonté
Ali House
AJ Ryan
Ellen Curtis
Erin Vance
Lauralana Dunne
Matthew LeDrew

PLAGUE OF THE DREAMLESS

JENNIFER SHELBY & JD RYOT

BOOKS

CHAPTER ONE

Cassidy lowered her voice to a desperate whisper, her knuckles whitening around her phone. "I'm getting cabin fever in here, Gamgee. It's just a cold."

"I understand your frustration, but I can't have you diving into potentially dangerous worlds if your reflexes are down. Admit it, you feel sluggish."

Cassidy refused to admit it, but she also knew her silence said as much. "At least send me a chaperone so I can go get some cold meds."

"I'll have cold medications sent to your hotel room. I'm not going to unleash an adrenaline junkie like Cassidy Cane into a country as restrictive as Saudi Arabia and hope for the best," said Gamgee. "Jubail isn't a tourist city like Dubai and you aren't a member of a respected archaeological team this trip. I don't mind paying bribes and pulling strings to get you out of a mess, but I'm sure as heck not rich enough to send you out there when you're already on the defensive. You've got to play by the rules in this country if you want to make it to the portal; any arrests and the owners will revoke their permission for you to visit their refinery. I had to throw a lot of dollar signs their way to get you that."

Cassidy didn't like it, but she knew he was right. "Fine."

"When you're feeling better, call the number I gave you. They'll arrange a chaperone to escort you from the hotel to the refinery portal. You have your abaya?"

"Yes." Cassidy glanced at the black polyester gown and head covering hanging over a chair in the hotel room. Local women were required to wear the gowns by law, but it would also serve Cassidy well sneaking through the refinery in the dark to find the portal.

"Good. Don't forget to stash it somewhere safe when you get to the other side of the portal. You'll need to be wearing it when you return. And Cassidy?"

"Yes?"

"I know it doesn't feel right, but for god's sake don't tell off any men while you're there."

Cassidy hung up and tossed her phone onto a nearby chair. It bounced half-heartedly and fell onto the thick carpet. Her sprawling hotel room was papered in a pearlescent Arabian design, the bed swimming in endless pillows. The massive jacuzzi tub was a wonder of bubbles and excess, but after two days of being cooped up with a cold and nothing but the WIFI to distract her, she was itching for something to happen. Anything to get her pulse going.

At last a knock sounded at her door. It must be the cold meds from Gamgee. Cassidy bounded to the door, reaching for the handle. She hesitated, glancing back to the abaya laid across the chair. She should put it on, and had put it on, albeit resentfully, when she accepted her room service meals, but darn it she needed a thrill, even a tiny one. She flung the door open, baring her face and hair to the world.

No one was there to see it. A small paper sack sat on the floor.

Cassidy sighed and snatched it up, closing the door behind her.

An hour later the cold medication cleared the lingering fog of her cold symptoms, but feeling better did little to settle her restlessness. She paced the room, resenting the way her toes sank deep into the luxurious carpet and how it muffled her furious stomps.

Enough of this nonsense. She felt fine. It was time to get to work. She dialled the number Gamgee had given her. A male voice greeted her. "This is Cassidy Cane," she said.

After a pause the voice told her, in English, "Put on the abaya. We'll be there in five minutes."

Cassidy grinned, shoving a few extra cold pills into her pocket just in case, and pulled her long, red hair into a ponytail.

***

Even in darkness the heat of the desert country was stifling, made a hundred times worse buried in swaths of black polyester. Cassidy peered over to the older woman acting as her chaperone. She seemed friendly enough, but had said nothing during the whole of the lengthy car ride. Neither had the driver. It was disconcerting, but Cassidy supposed that neither of them had any regular need to speak English and her broken Arabic did little to inspire lengthy conversation.

Cassidy turned her attention to the strange world coming into view beyond the car windows. A forest of tangled pipes crowded the horizon, broken only by the barrel-like squat of oil reservoirs. Here and there flare stacks belched a burst of flames into the sky. Strange to realize she hadn't left her home world yet.

Cassidy squinted at the map on her phone, a quick schematic of a single refinery marked with an arrow to indicate the position of a portal. It opened on the north side of a large silo, though where on that north side would be up to her to find. Gamgee had arranged for the security lights to be off until Cassidy completed her work, and swathed in the black abaya she should be able to travel unseen into the portal. Getting home would be another matter, but the uncertainty added to Cassidy's fun. Gosh, it was good to be free of that blasted hotel room.

The driver turned off the highway, pulling into the pipe forest. Far in the distance, the reservoirs sat, a scrawl of Arabic she couldn't read delineating one tank from another. Her driver appeared to know the area well, navigating with ease through the maze of repetitive structures.

The car stopped beside a reservoir painted white with a gold strip along the top. Cassidy's driver turned in his seat and nodded to her.

She opened the car door with a quickening pulse and tucked her phone securely into the pocket of the pants she wore beneath her abaya. Slinking into the shadows, she jogged to the reservoir. The structures were much bigger than they appeared from afar. She estimated this one to be at least six stories high and twice as wide around.

She circled the round structure, hunting for the telltale signs of a portal, usually revealed by a shimmer of light, but found nothing. On the north side of the structure there was nothing but darkness and a maintenance ladder. "Nowhere to go but up," Cassidy said to herself, leaping past the locked entry rungs and scrambling upward. The abaya tangled around her feet, tripping her up. Cassidy cursed and considered chucking the thing, but thought better of it. She'd need it to get home, after all. Instead, she pulled it up with one hand and tucked it into the waistband of her pants as best she could.

Six stories should have been an easy climb for her fitness level, but halfway up Cassidy felt sluggish, a slight stuffiness returning to her sinuses. Maybe she should have waited another day. No, dang it, she felt like a bird flapping against its cage, empty of every thought but her desperate need to escape.

She caught her breath and steadied herself on the ladder. Bursts of flames flashed in the distance, and something else, something white, flickered in the air just below her feet. Cassidy focused on the familiar light: the portal.

The portal was positioned a meter out, on the far side of the safety cage surrounding the ladder, and still some three stories high. Cassidy whistled.

It was quick work to climb down and back up along the outside of the cage. The heat pressed down on her, but she trusted her body to take her where she needed to be. She calculated the distance she would need to jump, climbing above the portal to give herself the right trajectory.

Gamgee would disapprove. He'd want her to check the portal, not dive headfirst into the unknown, but she had no tools on her person and she'd be damned if she was going to go back to that hotel room to await whatever Gamgee could scrounge up at the last minute.

Besides, her pulse was climbing already. She needed this. Her abaya and the darkness hid the wide grin splashed across her face, but her loud whoop echoed through the forest of pipes and reverberated against the reservoir walls as she leapt from the ladder and disappeared into the portal.

CHAPTER TWO

Cassidy exhaled slowly as the portal enveloped her body. A sensation of pressure weighed upon her skin. Holding her breath, she opened her eyes to a purple light. A group of burgundy, tentacled creatures the size of a tall building hung in the air. Whether they were giant squid, octopus, jellyfish, or all three, Cassidy couldn't say, though they were definitely some sort of cephalopod. The creatures stared at her with quiet power, their dark, oval pupils milky in the strange light. Cassidy forced herself to look away, dizzied and uncertain if it was the lack of oxygen or something else.

The nearest cephalopod reached out a tentacle lined with suction cups and flexing with lean muscle. Cassidy tried not to gag as it poked inside her mouth, prodding gently down her throat. The tentacle tasted of salt, a strange tingle leaving her mouth momentarily numb. She fought against the instinct to bite down, hoping the creature meant her no harm.

The tingling ceased when the beast removed its tentacle and probed inside her ears instead. Cassidy struggled to hide her annoyance. Were these cephalopods simply curious wild animals or sentient beasts who roamed a liminal space between dimensions? Either way, she'd soon need air ...getting lightheaded; and what did they want, anyway?

A deep fatigue overwhelmed her senses; she'd black out soon. The cephalopods blinked in unison and Cassidy slipped out of the portal.

A sweet burst of oxygen filled her lungs, air whooshing over her skin. Oh crap. She was falling. Cassidy flailed her arms, strange half-glimpses of patchwork skyscrapers and orange vapour filtering past the rush of adrenaline that left her giddy with misplaced glee.

Something scraped at her elbow and slammed into her armpit, jarring her shoulder joint and collar bone but giving her something to cling to. She ignored the pain, wrapping her legs up and around the pipe that caught her. Once secure, she gritted her teeth and, wincing, reached up to a smaller pipe sticking out of the brick to test her shoulder. Sore, but nothing broken or dislocated.

Sitting atop the pipe, she took a proper look at the world she'd entered. Jagged high-rises filled an industrial skyline. Floors the size of warehouses sat stacked on top of each other, chimneys and exhaust pipes sticking out along the sides, puffing orange smoke into the air. The horizon lay cloaked in rust-coloured clouds, the day a perpetual sunset. The air smelled of salt, yet acrid with old grease. Below her, several stories down, the orange smog gave way to a purple mist that hovered above the streets.

Cassidy peered to her right, sucking in her breath to see one of the cephalopods from the portal hanging in midair. In this light, she could make out flecks of burgundy along the soft milky flesh beneath the tentacles, bruising to a dark purple at the tips. She dared not meet the creature's eyes as it stared at her a long moment before closing its eyelids slowly, its body never moving.

"What are you?" Cassidy whispered to herself. She counted seven uneven stories in the building behind it. The cephalopods couldn't have made the buildings, she realized. The common architecture suggested the skyscrapers were the work of fellow humanoids. Did the two live in unison?

Cassidy shrugged off her questions. She needed to find a way off this perch. The portal shimmered above her, but she could see enough space to squeeze past, clinging to the building, if she could find handholds in the brick.

Brick struck her as an odd choice for a high-rise and odder still, each story in the buildings she could see were all built different from the last, as if every floor was unplanned. How could the original foundation support so many afterthoughts? Yet there they stood, reaching into the sky between sleeping sea monsters.

She refocused on the climb ahead. The mortar had crumbled in places, providing hand holds she could take advantage of, and an open window pushed out some ten meters above her perch, past the portal.

Heaving herself around to face the building, the pipe beneath her shifted, likely broken when it caught her. Cassidy hurried to her feet, pressing her body against the wall as she searched for toeholds to relieve the pipe. Her sturdy boots weren't the best footwear for such a task, but the sole at her toe fit snugly into the depression of mortar between the layers of brick. The abaya flapped in the wind around her like a misbehaved shadow, catching on bricks and pipes. Cassidy climbed steadily, holds revealing themselves as she got close to them.

Hot desert air breathed on her skin as she moved past the portal. It wasn't going to be easy getting home, three storeys in the air off an oil reservoir, but there was plenty of time to worry about that later.

She clutched the frame of the open window with her sore shoulder, aching in earnest now, and slipped inside as the first voices of this world reached her ears. Her hands slapped at the cool concrete floor and she somersaulted behind a long stack of palettes.

Cassidy pulled off the abaya and stuffed it into a palette for safekeeping. She strained to listen to what was being said across the room, squinting through the crates to see the speakers better. Their shape suggested humanoids, as she'd suspected. They had gathered near a rectangular machine the size of a minivan.

"Line up here. No talking," said a man in an officer-like uniform, his hand on a weapon he wore on his waist. Probably a handgun or a Taser, given the shape. His use of English irked Cassidy. She didn't expect to find another world which spoke English. That seemed extremely unlikely. Her stomach knotted. Something wasn't right.

Cassidy scowled at the group of people. She didn't like the way they were positioned, either. A handful of youth openly wept while the armed guards looked on, their expressions suggesting annoyance.

The lights overhead cut out and a large television screen flickered to life. A middle to late-aged man, his hair white and tidy, facial hair trimmed just so, gazed out at the room with practiced confidence. He smiled, his unnaturally perfect teeth flashing. "Happy birthday to the newest employee-citizens of Factorytown! I'm Bryce Bezanson, CEO of the Amazing Company and owner of Factorytown. Science has proven again and again that sixteen is the safest and most effective age to extract your imaginations, and today you have come of age. Congratulations!"

"What in the actual heck," murmured Cassidy. She took advantage of the televised distraction to creep closer to the group of huddled teenagers. A boy in a grey jacket turned to look her way, furrowing his brow. He was just a kid, large brown eyes, his face still smooth and feminine, dark hair tumbling across his features.

"By removing your imaginations, all employee-citizens of Factorytown are guaranteed to lead happy and productive lives without the dangerous and criminal distraction of daydreams. Rest assured, your imaginations will be put to good use: fed to the visionary engineers who will use them to create more and more of the Amazing Company's trademark transcendental technologies."

Cassidy cocked an ear. Gamgee would be interested in that kind of tech. This trip might be quicker than she thought.

Bezanson's lips stretched into a thin line, speaking through clenched teeth. "Let me remind you that Factorytown is the wholly owned subsidiary of the Amazing Company and any citizens living without compliance to Company Policy will be removed with extreme prejudice. Safety must be upheld."

The film skipped, Bezanson's position to the camera shifting to the left. His anger was gone, replaced by the same calculated composure as before. "Since implementing mandatory imagination extractions, workplace accidents have become non-existent, productivity has never been higher, and citizens' quality of life has skyrocketed."

"Liar," said grey-jacket boy, scowling at the screen. One of the officers pulled out a small club and pushed the boy to the front of the line.

Bezanson flashed a smug smile. "With your new, enhanced brains, you will be able to focus completely on the task at hand. Congratulations! You are about to become full-fledged staff members of the Amazing Company. Please approach the Imagination Extraction Device and complete your journey into your career!"

A woman in a pair of blue coveralls pulled a lever and the van-sized metal box, presumably the Imagination Extraction Device, groaned and creaked as the gears hidden behind its metal frame began to turn. "Him first, Rika." One of the officers shoved the boy in grey forward, forcing him toward a ragged chair made tiny by the machine looming around it. Strips of silver tape strained to hold the worn vinyl seat together while thick restraint braces protruded from the arms and legs of the chair. The boy paled as the officer shoved him into it. Rika, the lady in coveralls, fastened a belt brace about the boy's neck while the officers did the same to his hands and feet.

Rika squeezed the boy's hand once and pulled a branched dome down over the boy's head. She flicked a switch and the neural interface lit up as it hugged his skull. Thin yellow tubing ran from the electrodes of the interface to the belly of the machine.

Cassidy struggled with her conscience. She was here to steal tech, not save the world, but she could see the silver sheen of reflected light where the boy's silent tears tracked down his cheeks, disappearing into restraints that had probably absorbed far too many tears already. He hadn't consented to giving up his imagination: that Bezanson fellow had removed all choice from the matter with his 'mandatory compliance' nonsense.

Cassidy's mind made itself up. All eyes were on the boy, drinking in his terror. She took the chance and bounded up to the rear of the machine.

The welds, though crude, were strong along the box's edges. The only weakness Cassidy could see was an access panel the size of a small door with an intimidatingly large padlock barring any further exploration.

Thin, steel tubing ran from the IED to the exterior wall, a gash in the metal revealing a softer tube protected within, filled with a purple fog like she'd seen on the streets below. Cassidy prodded her fingers into the gash and pinched the soft tube closed. The tube jumped and swelled like she'd cut off suction. She saw nothing else connected to the machine; could this be its power supply? Cassidy tugged a length from its protective sheath and tied a quick knot in the tubing.

The IED coughed and wheezed, the knot she'd tied lifting off the floor as it fought for breath or fuel. A long creak sounded from within the metal box, followed by a zinging bang.

There was a small moment of nothing, and then smoke

poured out around the access panel. The building's fire alarm went off without hesitation.

The guards and youth on the far side of the machine ran for the exits as the sprinkler systems spat a half-hearted burst of grimy water and fell silent.

Cassidy dashed for the boy still strapped to the extraction device, surprised to find Rika still there, undoing the boy's restraints. "Stay still till I get you out, Merrick," she told the boy. The interface over Merrick's head was still lit up, his eyes wide with fear as smoke slowly filled the room. Cassidy tackled the leg restraints while Rika switched off the buttons on the interface.

He remained still until Rika lifted the halo, then he leapt from the ragged seat and cast a grimace towards the extraction device. Cassidy met his eye and gave him a lopsided grin.

"Run, you idiots!" hissed Rika.

CHAPTER THREE

Merrick grabbed Cassidy's arm, pulling her along as he dashed towards a dark hole in the wall opposite the one she'd come in from. "Trust me, this is the best way out," he told her when she stopped cold. He released her hand and launched himself, feet first, into the tunnel.

Cassidy hesitated, but the steady stomp of footfalls behind her sent her sliding down behind him. The chute twisted and looped, its bottom uneven. Someone far above shouted, the sound bouncing off the dark chute in unison with her body until it deposited her atop a lumpy pile of blue coveralls.

"Grab a pair and come on," said Merrick, his hair falling across his frightened face.

"Who are we running from?" asked Cassidy, reaching for the coveralls.

He threw a pair over his shoulder. "Compliance Officers."

Cassidy followed him down an alley, wisps of purple fog swirling in their wake. The streets were cobblestone and slippery with a mildewed, perpetual damp, the sun long blocked from reaching the ground. The only living thing Cassidy saw was a few sprigs of orange lichen clinging to the cobbles.

The boy led her through a maze of alleyways and crumbling ground floors propped up by joists and stacks of rotten brick. Most of these lower levels were abandoned for the churning, thumping upper factories. The machines towering overhead vibrated through the foundation, small showers of dust and debris falling at regular intervals. Here and there someone crouched or slept within the dim light of these dubious shelters.

Cassidy struggled to take note of the route they were taking, as she'd need to find the portal home later, but the boy dodged through the city with the ease of the familiar and everything was new to her. Shouts from behind let her know that someone—had he called them Compliance Officers?—were still in pursuit.

Cassidy and Merrick ran up a flight of stairs, the bright lights and industrial rhythm of a working factory blasting through her senses. Cassidy's adrenaline spiked with a dizzying euphoria and her thoughts narrowed into strict details. The tingling scent of the steaming dye vats. The thump of a loom shuttle. The whir of unspooling thread. A door slamming behind them. Another shout, running. The smash of her own footsteps against a metal walkway. Endless rows of rattling sewing machines spewing out below, workers dressed in the same blue uniform she held tight against her chest.

The boy ran on, never pausing, though in the foul air Cassidy's lungs ached. A row of doors appeared ahead, Merrick peering back at their pursuers before clutching her hand and pulling her through an opened one.

"Quickly, put the covvies on." He zipped his pair over his clothes. "I'm Merrick," he added, shuffling to a second door on the other side of the closet. He cracked it open, filling the space with light.

"Cassidy."

"Thanks for saving me back there, Cassidy." He pointed to a group of similarly coveralled employees milling around an open break room. "They're heading back to work. If we slip into the group as they go by, we might be able to sneak off this floor without the officers seeing us."

"Okay," Cassidy agreed. "And what exactly happens if they do catch us?"

"They'll turn you over to the Dreamkeeper." He said the word as if it filled him with dread.

He signalled for her to come closer and they slipped into the workers' midst. The employees eyed them with curiosity but said nothing.

Below, the officers from the imagination extraction made their way between the sewing machines. One of the officers looked Cassidy's way, but they didn't recognize her. Cassidy doubted they'd seen much of her at all. Merrick, on the other hand... "What about you? Are they after you, too?"

"I'm not sure," he answered, eyeing the officers himself. "I don't think they saw me leave. If they think my extraction was completed, they won't be interested in me at all."

"Did they complete the extraction?"

"Nope, thanks to you." Merrick grinned, a wide, happy thing. "Where did you come from? You just appeared."

Cassidy shrugged. "A few towns over."

"Shippingsburg?"

"Um, yeah." The moment the words left her mouth, she regretted them.

"It is true that the Underground there has access to dream dust?" His eyes were serious, intent. This meant something to him.

Cassidy swallowed. The employees had quieted their chatter, listening for her answer. Lying had been a bad idea, but the truth wasn't much better. "Maybe. Why?"

"I've got an aunt in the last stages of the plague. If you know of any way I could get dream dust to save her, it would mean a lot."

Plague? A sweat prickled at Cassidy's underarms. What had she just walked into? The factory workers glanced over to her, openly hopeful. "I'm sorry. I'd help if I could, but I don't know."

The air hung heavier than it had before. Merrick's brow creased as the group reached the factory floor and splintered. Cassidy and Merrick moved through an exterior door that opened to a fire escape winding downward, a bulge in the walls of the first floor obvious from their vantage point. Cassidy shuddered. The entire high-rise should have collapsed a long time ago.

On the ground in the now-familiar mist, Cassidy tried to get her bearings, but the city was a hopeless jumble: buildings built haphazard and without any real streets she could make out. She felt a pang of longing for a tree.

Sneaking down another alley, the sky suddenly opened to reveal a cephalopod. Cassidy held back, staring, waiting for it to open its eyes. "What are those things?" she asked.

Merrick followed her gaze. "What, the Engineer? You don't have Engineers in Shippingsburg?"

Cassidy sighed. "I'm sorry, I'm not from Shippingsburg. I shouldn't have lied to you, but it's not easy to explain. Can we just say I'm visiting from afar and leave it at that?"

"For the lady who rescued me from extraction? Absolutely. You get a free pass for life." He gave her a silly wink. "Come on, there's a broken 'scraper up ahead, we'll be safe there. Compliance Officers don't like going inside."

This time he led her toward a high-rise leaning at a severe angle, held up by grace of the two buildings that stopped its fall. The chimneys and exhausts pipes lay idle, it's factories long since abandoned.

To her horror, Merrick scrambled up the leaning building. "Merrick, that isn't safe." She could risk her life, fine, but she didn't like the idea of this kid risking his, not for her.

He winked at her. "Scared?"

"Kid, if you only knew the stuff I've done."

"It's safe. The Engineers keep it from falling."

"Those cephalopods?"

"Yeah." He gestured farther up the building. "There used to be a cannery up there years ago, when I was a kid. We can find something to eat."

"Don't you have a home, a family, someone who makes you dinner?"

His posture sagged as he shook his head. "The plague

got them a year ago. Dad didn't last long after Mom died. They arranged for me to stay with my aunt, but she's..."

"She's the one you mentioned earlier, the one in the last stages of plague." Cassidy studied his face for signs of grief, but youthful skin didn't tell the same stories as older folks.

"That's right." His expression darkened for a moment before he forced a weak smile. "Now come on, it'll be dark soon and I'm hungry."

The orange sky had dimmed some, though Cassidy doubted the night in this industrial place would be much darker than Jubail had been under its myriad of security lights. She climbed the building, the angle steep enough to be challenging and the strange perspective of walking up the side of a Leaning Skyscraper of Pisa worth making a memory of. Insta-worthy, even. She chuckled to herself, working hard to climb steadily, imagining Gamgee's reaction to posting her inter-dimensional exploits on Instagram. When Merrick wasn't looking, she pulled the phone Gamgee gave her from inside her coveralls and snapped a few quick shots. Of course, she'd never post them anywhere, she just wanted the small thrill of rebellion and its accompanying endorphins.

CHAPTER FOUR

Some dozen storeys later, Merrick slid open a window and showed Cassidy a rope attached to the frame they could climb down. Street kids could be counted on to know all the best places, no matter what dimension you were in, she supposed, wishing she could do more for him.

"If your extraction was successful, would you have a job in the factories?" Cassidy asked him.

"Yeah. I may still, if they think it worked. I'll check in tomorrow and see if I have an assignment."

She waited while he climbed down the rope and found his footing below. "And once you have a job, you'll be able to find a place to live?"

He blew on his hands, hot from friction, and kicked at the debris at his feet. "All workers get assigned barracks and food cards."

"Bezanson provides everything?" Cassidy asked, descending slowly and wishing for a pair of gloves as the rope seared her palms and the ache in her shoulder reawakened.

Merrick dug out a few unlabelled cans from a tangle of broken crates and tucked them into the pockets of his coveralls. "They don't provide dreams," he muttered, anger in his voice.

Cassidy fished out a can of her own. "Provide for the body, not the mind."

"The companies make it seem like a good thing—the shelter, the food—but I've been out here a few months on my own and I'm fine." He threw a bloated, dented can to the far end of the room. It crashed against a conveyor belt, the sound echoing through the room. "I don't need them."

"Then why show up for extraction at all? Why not run?"

He stared across the cannery, a haunted expression on his face. "Because we get three free dream tokens when we get our first work assignment."

"And you wanted to save your aunt."

Merrick nodded and shifted a crate to the side, revealing a fresh trove of cans. "Sweet!" He handed her one and replaced the crate.

Cassidy gave him a questioning look.

"Any more than two without a backpack and we're not going to be able to climb out of here," he told her. "Besides, the next kid up here will be hungry too."

Cassidy climbed the rope first, helping Merrick crawl over the awkward windowsill. She noticed a small, palm-sized brown flag a few stories above. "What is that?" Cassidy asked.

Merrick hesitated. "Can I trust you?"

She kept her gaze on the flag. "Probably not."

He lifted his head in shock, not recognizing it as a joke until he met her eyes. "Fair enough, you did save me back there. That," he gestured to the window by the flag, "is Resistance headquarters." He climbed up to the window and pushed it open. "Just popping in before nightfall," he said loudly, and slipped inside.

A makeshift ladder descended into the darkness below. Once inside, Merrick led Cassidy past a blackout curtain and into a room which made her head ache. The floor, monstrously tilted from its collapse, had makeshift scaffolding set up to straighten the severe angle of the original floor. A small laboratory sat atop the scaffolding, its technology recognizable.

"We call this building Nightfall," Merrick told her. "The Resistance works to get dreams to those who need them."

"But undermining the dream economy is the ultimate goal," said a beautiful young woman with a sleek robot suit strapped over her limbs, a similar neural interface to the one used in the imagination extractions hugging her head.

"This is Minseo," said Merrick, "She's fourteen, still has her imagination, and she's also a chemistry genius."

"I'm not a genius." Minseo rolled her eyes, a faint blush on her cheeks as she gave Merrick a shy glance. "I'm trying to reverse engineer the dream dust, so we can bypass the Dispensary altogether. If I was a genius, it would already be done, but I'm not, so here we are."

"It's more than I could do," said Cassidy, trying hard not to stare at the girl's robot suit.

"My parents are both chemists as well," said Minseo,

catching Cassidy's confused smile. "That's how they were able to get me a suit before I'm of useful age. I'm one of the lucky ones."

"Useful?" Cassidy glanced at Merrick.

"Cassidy's not from Factorytown," said Merrick.

"Oh?" Minseo's expression turned to one of deep interest. "Where are you from?"

"She's not telling and it's very mysterious, but she saved me from my extraction and if I'm not mistaken…" Merrick raised an eyebrow and winked at Cassidy. "She still has her imagination."

Minseo's eyes grew wide, her robot-supported fingers twitching. "Oh my gosh, how is that possible?"

"She's not telling," Merrick answered for her again. "But I trust her. Is that good enough for you, Min?"

The girl nodded, giving Cassidy a curious look.

Cassidy crossed her arms. "Where do you get the samples of dust to reverse engineer?"

"We had a source close to the Dreamkeeper who smuggled them out to us, but she's been missing for several weeks. We're more than a little worried she got caught, but we're still able to run simulations based on those former samples. The trouble is that there are elements in the dust that we don't recognize and can't source naturally." Minseo sighed. "Which is unfortunately common when the Engineers' technomagic is involved."

A processor behind Minseo beeped and she turned, obviously distracted. "We'll let you get back to work," said Merrick. "I'm just showing Cassidy around. Tell the others if you can, we have a new ally."

Minseo nodded and held up her hand in a half-hearted wave, scarcely looking up from her work.

Cassidy waited until they were back on the outside of the Nightfall building before she asked. "Why was she wearing a robot suit?"

"Why? I don't know, I thought it rude to ask," said Merrick.

"Rude? Is she a cyborg?"

"No," said Merrick slowly. "It's a suit connected to her brain, allowing her to use her body to its full potential."

Cassidy struggled to make sense of what he said. Why would she need that—oh. "Wait, is the suit an accessibility device for someone with disabilities?"

"That's a strange way to say it, but yeah, essentially. The neural interface can replace damaged biological elements, like a severed limb or spinal cord."

Cassidy's mind raced. Gamgee would love to get his hands on something like that. "How does it work?"

"The Engineers make them work," he said, a trace of sadness in his tone. "The more they sleep the more we stand to lose."

She wanted to ask him what that meant, but she didn't want to change the subject yet. "Where could I get one of those suits?"

Merrick shrugged and held up his hands as if in surrender. "It's not that easy. Each one has to be calibrated to the user's brainwaves, which takes a long time, and the cost is astronomical."

Maybe not this trip, then. Cassidy filed the knowledge into the back of her mind in case she ever needed it.

"Let's go," said Merrick. "I don't want to be up here all night. We can stay in the plague room on the lower level for the night. We'll be safe there."

"Plague room? That doesn't sound like it's safe from the plague."

"You can't catch the plague, it's not contagious." He froze, his eyes widening. "You don't have the plague of the dreamless where you're from?"

He whistled when she shook her head. "Wow. Well, don't worry, because if you've still got your imagination, you can't get the plague and neither can I."

CHAPTER FIVE

The shadows were darker near the bottom of Nightfall, creating an atmosphere of secret and mystery. Unseen people shuffled in those shadows as Merrick and Cassidy entered the crumbling first floor, a grim space lit only by a garbage can fire in its centre and the dwindling light of day. The faces Cassidy glimpsed were dirty, hungry, and haunted. Some, perhaps sicker than the others, huddled under ratty blankets, pressed against the walls, noticeably twitching, an air of desperation aching in their eyes.

The scent of unwashed bodies did little to mask the pungent decay of the building itself; mushrooms blooming on wooden shelves, a pool of brackish, oily water seeping mildew in its wake as it gathered up the weeping damp.

Merrick chose a dry-ish bit of empty floor and sat, pulling a can opener from somewhere in his coveralls and attacking one of his cans. "Pasta! You're in luck," he declared, handing it to Cassidy.

She peered inside at the canned spaghetti she might have loved if she were still twelve. Still, looking around at the dirty faces past the firelight, she wouldn't waste it. "I think the sick need it more than I do."

Merrick shook his head. "They won't eat, they're tweaking; all they want is a dream. You should eat. We don't have any way to get meal tickets so long as we still have our imaginations. Eat when you can," he said, slurping at a can of peas he'd opened for himself.

Cassidy tried the cold spaghetti. It wasn't awful, and she was hungry. "Can you tell me more about this plague?"

"Will you tell me where you're really from?"

Cassidy thought it over. "Maybe. If you help me."

"Works for me. What you do you want to know?"

"You said the plague is caused by a lack of dreams?"

"Right. You see, after our imaginations are extracted, we're no longer capable of dreaming, but it turns out our brains need dreams to work properly. And without them, our brains slowly break down."

Cassidy slurped at her spaghetti, flecks of sauce splattering onto her coveralls. "And this transcendental tech stuff is worth this kind of sacrifice?"

"Maybe. I've never seen any of the tech Bezanson's always talking about, but I'm the son of factory workers, we were never wealthy."

"But surely you've heard of it, seen it somewhere. Has Minseo ever mentioned it?" Cassidy chewed the cold noodles thoughtfully. Beyond Minseo's suit she hadn't seen anything remotely transcendent in this broken down city.

"Well, the Engineers built the city and they power our factories," Merrick said, faltering.

But the factories looked old, dingy, and worn out. Cassidy decided not to point that out to him. "Then why do it? If you get nothing from this, why comply?"

"Legend has it," Merrick began.

"Legend?"

He shrugged. "There's no one left alive from back then. The plague gets most people in middle-age." He sighed. "When the extractions first started, the Engineers were active, not dormant like they are now. People adored them and were happy to share. Only now, the Dreamkeeper and the CEOs control the dream dust and every year the price of dreams gets higher. Now everyone is working for dreams. The cities belong to the CEOs who dole out rooms, food, and wages in exchange for absolutely everything we have, and after we're bled dry, we end up here." He gestured around the room. "To die."

"And the Resistance?" Cassidy stared hard at the boy.

He shook his head. "It's not enough. Even if Minseo can reverse engineer the dust, Bezanson still controls the ingredients."

The room grew dark as the sun disappeared from the sky. One by one, the lights shut off across the city. "The CEOs shut the power grid down after the factories close, to save electricity," said Merrick.

Someone in the shadows behind him tossed a pair of coveralls onto the fire, dampening the embers a moment before the fabric whooshed aflame. Cassidy chewed her lip. These people deserved better.

"So, where'd you say you were from again?" asked Merrick.

Cassidy's nose twitched, her sinuses suddenly seizing.

The sneeze ripped out of her before she had the chance to tuck her face into her elbow. She shook her head to clear it. "Sorry, that snuck up on me."

"Are you okay?" Merrick's voice sounded concerned.

"I'm fine, just getting over a cold."

"Cold? Let's stand closer to the fire, would you like my coat?" he asked.

"No, no, a cold, not I'm cold. But thank you, that's very sweet." She ignored his confused look. The renewed firelight highlighting the miserable faces tucked into the shadows. "So all anyone in here needs to get better is a single dream?"

A sick man across the room met her eyes and nodded. "And this Dreamkeeper fellow," she continued, "is okay with people dying because they can't afford a dream that they should be entitled to by dint of forced brain surgery?"

"The Dreamkeeper likes to watch people suffer," warned Merrick, his voice low. "It gives him pleasure."

Cassidy rubbed her eyes. Nothing in this bleak dystopia made sense. "Let's go back a bit. How does that machine back there work? How can it extract a person's imagination?"

Merrick gave her a bemused look. "You really don't know anything, do you?"

"Not from around here, remember?"

"I'll say. The Imagination Extraction Device is enhanced with the Engineers' technomagic."

"How?"

Merrick shrugged. "Sorry, I don't know anything about that. All I do know is that the technomagic makes the machines do what they are designed to do. It fixes any flaws, powers it, and repairs the machine when it breaks."

Cassidy glanced around the caved-in room. "And that's what keeps these buildings from crushing each other?"

"Exactly."

Cassidy watched his face, waiting for signs that he knew something was wrong, that these buildings were breaking, that the machines were barely holding on to functionality. Everything here was on the cusp of falling apart. But he was young, she reminded herself, he may not have known it any other way. And if the older people were systematically being killed off, then no one ever would.

"Minseo could explain the science to you in more detail," said Merrick.

"I'll have to ask her," she told him. "Because this place is bewildering."

"Compared to what?"

"Would you believe me if I told you I'm an alien from another dimension?" asked Cassidy.

Merrick looked thoughtful in the firelight. "Fair enough. Any other weird questions you'd like to ask me?"

He was taking this rather well. "What do you call your world?"

"Cephalon."

"Okay. And what do you call yourselves?"

"People."

Huh. His answers irked Cassidy. This wasn't Earth.

The odds that they called themselves the same English word were ridiculous. Unless they were a splinter group of humanity with convergent evolution... but even then, the likelihood was less than slim. "How many genders does your species have?"

Merrick considered the question a long moment. "Four? Male, female, neither, and both. I could be missing some. My experience is limited. Anything else?"

Impossible. Unless— "Do you get a lot of visitors from other dimensions and planets here?"

"There's an old story my father liked to tell, one he said he learned from his dad, that sort of thing. In this story, we were refugees without a planet. No home, just lost and drifting in outer space until the Engineers found us and shared their world with us."

"You're the aliens, then."

Merrick nodded. Cassidy gestured to the darkness past the building. "Does the story say what this world was like when you first got here?"

"No factories," Merrick answered, sitting cross-legged, his voice distant. "An endless purple fog unbroken by 'scrapers and a myriad of Engineers active in the sky."

"Are they sick, too?" asked Cassidy. "Is that why they're always asleep?"

"I don't know," said Merrick. "One day they just stopped, hanging there, like they were waiting for something."

"Waiting?"

"Yeah. Don't you think they look like they're waiting?"

"I don't know about that," said Cassidy. She shook

her head, struggling to unite this new information of the cephalopods with her impression of the ones she met inside the portal. Neither the cephalopods there nor the one watching when she arrived here had been asleep. She shivered, trying to shake the uncomfortable feeling that they were watching her even now.

The night fell quiet as the fire's fuel ran low. The dreamless shifted into a small heap to sleep, holding hands like children. She noticed Merrick watching, too.

"Comfort," he said quietly. He stretched out on the ground and tucked up his arm for a pillow. "Sorry I can't offer you anywhere nicer on your first visit to Factorytown."

Cassidy smirked, saying nothing. The fire would be out soon, its glow and crackle a comfort. Strange to imagine the Engineers hanging in the darkness somewhere overhead. She wondered if the smog made them sick as it blocked out the stars, or if they breathed at all.

Rats or worse shuffled in the shadows as she shut her eyes. This was a hardscrabble life. If she wanted to get her hands on any tech, she needed richer neighbourhoods, wherever they might be.

The fire snuffed out, the darkness complete. Merrick began to snore lightly, holding her in this world as an anchor while her imagination unspooled with all the worlds she'd visited, and sleep stole away the night.

CHAPTER SIX

Cassidy awoke to a world thick with purple mist, the dreamless already awake and gone, Merrick snoring fitfully. She sat up, stretching out the aches of sleeping rough. From the broken window she spotted long rows of workers heading to their factories, a sea of blue coveralls.

Many wiped sleep from bleary eyes, but no one smiled. The joy had been sucked dry from these people, and it tugged at Cassidy's conscience. There had to be something she could do.

She could start with the Dreamkeeper, learn what she could. Go from there. If nothing else, he was the immediate barrier to these people's happiness.

She leaned past the broken windowsill, flinching as she saw an Engineer's tentacle from the corner of her eye. It must have moved there in the night. Shaking off her discomfort, she stepped outside, hands stuffed in her coveralls. Gosh, she could use some coffee, but all she found in her pockets was her pocketknife, a few tablets of cold medication, and the can of food from last night.

She peered up the half-collapsed high-rise, the early

morning shadows tinged purple from the heavy mist that had replenished itself overnight. There was not one, but three massive cephalopods hanging above, shifting in the colour spectrum from blue to purple. Their tentacles appeared to fall downward, but at this vantage Cassidy could see their long muscles flexing. The larger, outer tentacles had undersides dotted with suction cups Cassidy tried not to imagine squeezing around objects or squishing the life from her bones.

"Good morning," Merrick rubbed his forehead as he walked over to her. He froze when noticed the cephalopods overhead. "Whoa. They never move."

Cassidy had been worried about that. First the portal, now here. Were they tracking her? Warning? Or just keeping an eye on her? She looked to Merrick, biting back the questions she knew he couldn't answer. His skin tone was paler than it was yesterday, his eyes puffy.

"My head feels like it's overstuffed," he said.

"You did have a partial, magical brain surgery yesterday," said Cassidy, her tone light, but she didn't like the way he looked. "You okay?"

"I'm sure I can power through, but I feel strange." He straightened his posture as if to prove his words. "What are your interdimensional sight-seeing plans for today?"

Cassidy chuckled. "You really are taking that revelation well."

"I promise, I'm struggling on the inside. There's no shortage of weirdos here on Cephalon. Our imaginations are short, their expiration dates clearly stamped, and we have to make the most of what we've got, before and after."

"Fair enough," said Cassidy. "I'd like to see this Dreamkeeper fellow today."

Merrick startled, but recovered quickly. "He'll be at the Dispensary."

"Merrick? Is that you?" someone interrupted.

Merrick embraced an older woman who was clearly sick with plague. Her twitching body shivered with it, her expression hollow and desperate. "Aunt Tristine." He broke away and held her hand in his. "Something went wrong with the IED. I can't say for sure if I'll get my tokens today or not."

Tristine's lower lip wobbled, but the woman forced a smile. "You've still got your imagination, though?"

Merrick nodded.

"Maybe you'll be able to keep it," she said in a whisper, glancing around to see if anyone might hear. Her hands shook as she took them back, bulging into fists she pushed into her pockets. Her mouth pressed just enough to reveal the lie in her words and the guilt she felt for her own disappointment.

"I'll find some tokens for you somehow if I don't get any. There's still hope," Merrick told her.

Tristine pushed her lips into a smile. "Of course, and I love you either way." She turned to go, meeting Cassidy's eyes for a brief moment. Cassidy stepped back, overwhelmed by the bitter hopelessness in the woman's eyes.

Merrick watched her go with a furrowed brow before he turned back to Cassidy. "I've got to check and see if my work assignment and tokens have come in. Fingers crossed."

Cassidy nodded. "Be careful, it could still be a trap if

the Compliance Officers were onto you. If you notice any-thing out of the ordinary, get out of there."

"I will. And you be careful, too. Word will have gotten around that a red headed woman blew up the extraction device; the Officers might be checking anyone with that description to make sure they're proper citizens."

"How would I prove I'm a proper citizen?"

"Comply. You would never do anything to risk your next dream."

Merrick stepped out of his coveralls, revealing the grey jacket he'd been wearing when she first saw him in line for extraction. He was a good kid, Cassidy decided. He'd helped her, fed her, and in some small way helped her through her first night here. She'd hate to see anything happen to him because of her. "If you do get your assign-ment, when would you begin?"

"Tomorrow. I'll be back here tonight either way, be-cause if I get my tokens I'll need to find Aunt Tristine." He paused, unsure of himself. "Any chance we'll run into each other again?"

"I don't want to get you into any trouble," said Cassi-dy. "And I expect I'll be making some trouble."

Merrick grinned, swiping at his nose. "Come on, I'm heading across the factory district. There are several Dis-pensary tentacles along the way."

"Tentacles?"

He hadn't exaggerated. On almost every block lay what Merrick called a dream button: a tarnished gold cir-cle embedded into the cobblestones. The Dream Dispen-sary itself was located in a hot air balloon hovering over the city's high-rises. The balloon proper echoed the shape of an Engineer, painted to match the burgundy tones of their skin and the bruised grey around their ever-sleeping eyes. The style of the artwork reminded Cassidy of comic books back on Earth. Judging by the height and the detail Cassidy could still make out from the street, the balloon must be massive.

A middle-aged, dark haired man stepped onto a dream button as she watched. A flap unrolled from the ship beneath the balloon, a flowing false tentacle that curled around the man's waist and snatched him up into the belly of the air ship.

"You've got to be kidding me," said Cassidy.

Merrick chuckled. "Beats dying of plague. The Engineers are a symbol of peace and friendship, it's meant to put customers at ease."

Cassidy shuddered. The Engineers did anything but put her at ease. "Have you ever been up there?"

"No, dream dust is pretty dangerous if you have an imagination, so be careful. Everyone knows someone who knows a kid who got into their parents' dream stash. Their parents or sibling would find them, brain dead, blood trickling from their nose and ears. People used to be able to take the dust in a cup of tea before bed, but nowadays the Dreamkeeper administers it before anyone can leave the Dispensary to cut down on kids getting hurt. They claim that's why they put the Dispensary in an air ship, too, but I think it's got more to do with security and controlling who goes in and out."

"Controlled substance," murmured Cassidy, staring upward.

"Yeah." Merrick squinted with her. "Be careful up

there. I wouldn't know how to send you home again if you end up dead and I owe you that much. And watch out for the Dreamkeeper. He doesn't like loiterers very much.

"I'll keep that in mind."

Merrick sneezed, catching it in his hand at the last moment, a bewildered expression on his face. He stared at his wet hand as Cassidy turned away, to save him any embarrassment.

"If I don't run into you again, thank you for your help," she said, stepping onto the dream button.

The false tentacle whistled as it tumbled downward and wrapped around Cassidy's waist. The moment she felt the small pressure of it coiling tight, her feet left the ground and she went spiralling upward. Cassidy grinned. Though ridiculous, it was an undeniably fun means of travel. The factories below spun around her as she rose through the orange sky that tumbled through her vision. Strong winds buffeted against her face until a dark shadow swallowed her whole and she found herself inside the Dream Dispensary.

CHAPTER SEVEN

The false tentacle fell limp to the floor, coiling itself to wait for its next customer as Cassidy stepped out of it. She gripped the sides of the hatch as the balloon swayed in the fierce winds and peered outside, automatically seeking her only landmarks, Nightfall and the Engineers. More than one collapsed building lay on the ground. Factories spewed endless orange exhaust waste as the morning's purple mist visibly thinned.

She counted no less than eight cephalopods from her vantage point: the cluster of three from that morning, and one just below the Dispensary that hadn't been there when she'd been on the ground. The remaining four clustered around a teetering high-rise swaying in the heavy winds. No exhaust fumes billowed from the building, nor did it hold the strange, too-tall warehouse stories of the others. This looked more like an apartment complex back home. Maybe it was the barracks Merrick had spoken of.

Her stomach churned as the building swayed too far, a puff of dust rising from crumbled bricks, faces suddenly running to the windows, opening them wide, leaning out, their shapes too small to be adults.

Cassidy glanced around the strange entryway for something, anything, she could use to help, finding nothing. She turned back to the building in horror. Another gust of wind heaved the structure and she caught her breath as it leaned at an angle far too extreme to escape gravity, certain it was about to collapse like Nightfall had. Just as it should have fallen, the four cephalopods exuded a vast plume of purple fog that surrounded the building, setting it right. Cassidy could still feel the wind on her face, but the building swayed no more, solidified by whatever the Engineers had done with their strange mist.

She leaned against the wall of the Dispensary's entry hatch. Most adrenaline rushes were fun, but this was not one of them. The burgundy and blue creatures hovering over the city had saved that building, of that she had no doubt. She just wished she knew if it was out of kindness or the necessary maintenance of one's crop of human imagination. The idea unsettled her.

She had a Dreamkeeper to meet, she reminded herself, turning back into the Dispensary. The hatch had smooth, chrome-coated walls, well-polished and worn at the corners. A large, framed drawing of a man in a crimson coat grinned from its place on the chrome wall. The floor had a living quality to it, a three-dimensional glisten that gave the impression of walking on water as she stepped forward. Cassidy tried not to feel agog of it, remembering Merrick's warning of the danger present. She passed through a hallway lined with more comic book style drawings of the same man, up a small set of stairs, and into the Dispensary proper.

At the top of the stairs she found a round room with shelves and counters piled high with thousands of small, colourful bottles. The walls were painted the red of fresh blood, assaulting Cassidy's senses, now accustomed to industrial gloom. In the centre of the room stood the man from the drawings, the Dreamkeeper himself, adorned with a heavily embroidered, tailed jacket that matched the walls.

He glanced up at Cassidy as she entered the room, his face greasy with sweat, shadowed with stubble, and eyes too quick to wink. In the centre of the ring sat a bespectacled, middle-aged woman, her face lined with worry, her shoulders slumped with the weight of her world, her eyes never leaving the Dreamkeeper's face as he pranced from one shelf of bottles to the next.

"How's about a beach location? And oh, here, a dollop of sunshine. We've got ourselves a bona fide summer romance in the making, no guilt required." He poured a little of the glowing dust from each bottle into a tube he held tight in his fist. The dust inside glowed brighter as it shivered from the bottles to the tube. His fingers, Cassidy noted, were stained with splotches of black ink.

"Do you have anything that might cast off my inhibitions?" asked the woman. "I really need to relax. Let the stress go for a little while."

"Sure, sure," purred the Dreamkeeper. He wriggled his stained fingers over the bottles, making a show of selecting the perfect one from his collection.

Cassidy crossed her arms and watched, his every gesture exaggerated, his movements graceful, his voice booming and singsong as he spoke. The Dreamkeeper hunted for ingredients back and forth across the floor, his coattails taking flight behind him. He mixed the ingredients into a bullet-like tube, working with deft, powerful gestures and licking his lips, clearly salivating with anticipation.

In one deft movement, the Dreamkeeper pulled a large handgun from a hidden holster behind his crimson coat. He shoved the dream tube into its magazine, arced his arm over his head and pressed the barrel against the woman's temple. Cassidy froze.

"Say please," said the Dreamkeeper in his sing-song voice.

The woman giggled, her hands a-flutter. "Please."

The Dreamkeeper squeezed the trigger, the report of the gunshot echoing off the painted walls, the now-empty tube skittering across the floor to Cassidy's feet. The woman rubbed her temple and got to her feet. "Oh, thank you, Dreamkeeper," she babbled as she collected her purse.

Cassidy bent to retrieve the capsule. "I'll take that," said the Dreamkeeper, striding over and snatching it from Cassidy's hand.

Cassidy bristled with sudden loathing. "You like shooting people in the head?"

He laughed, a fake, theatrical thing. "All a part of the experience, my dear. What is sleep but a little death, in the end? After the first few hundred times, it loses its ability to disturb."

Cassidy whistled, walking around to put a table of bottles between them. "That's some over-the-top villainy right there."

The Dreamkeeper ran his fingers along the hot barrel of his gun and pressed his lips in a hard line. "I am not accustomed to being questioned in my methods."

"I suppose not. Head office sent me," lied Cassidy.

"I'm sure. And you have nothing to do with the strange, red-headed woman my Compliance Officers were chasing yesterday?"

Cassidy smiled as wide as her cheeks would allow. "Of course not."

His jaw clenched, but then something behind Cassidy distracted his attention away from her. His manner turned predatory, teeth bared, muscles taut, a growl rising from his throat. "You'd better have a dream token this time."

Cassidy turned to see Merrick's aunt standing behind her, body bent, twisted, the expression in her eyes more desperate than Cassidy remembered. The woman didn't notice Cassidy, intent upon the bottles. She rushed toward them, hands reaching to clutch at any bottle, eyes wide at the wealth of life-saving medicine laid out on the tables.

The Dreamkeeper was on Tristine in an instant, backhanding the woman before Cassidy knew what was happening. Tristine flipped over, landing on her hip, moaning. "How dare you steal from me!" he roared. His left leg rose to kick the older woman's belly when Cassidy threw herself at him, sending him off balance and tumbling into a table of dream dust bottles.

Colourful glass bottles shattered all around him, sending up puffs of blue dust that set him to panic. The Dreamkeeper leapt to his feet, taking off his crimson coat and throwing it to the floor in horror. *Dream dust was a danger to anyone with an imagination*, Merrick had said.

Tristine snatched a half-broken bottle as it rolled her way, spilling a small trail of blue glowing dust. Cassidy flinched as the woman gulped down what dust remained, paying no heed to the glass shards that were surely within.

Cassidy grabbed a few bottles and shoved them into the large pockets of her coveralls. She'd blown whatever small cover of anonymity she'd had; she might as well steal what she could while the Dreamkeeper wasn't looking.

A small gasp pulled her attention back to Tristine. The Dreamkeeper sat on the older woman's chest, gun in hand, his eyes filled with rage. "How dare you play the hero, how dare you steal from me!" he roared, smashing the butt of his gun down into Tristine's temple.

Cassidy grabbed at the largest bottle of dream dust within reach, pulled out its cork, and flung it at the man. It hit his gun, poised for another strike, and rained down a shower of blue. He dropped the weapon and rolled out of the dust, struggling to get to his feet. Spasming with fits of coughing, he threw his arm over his mouth and nose and stumbled down the stairs toward the tentacle hatches.

Tristine lay still. Cassidy lobbed a few more open bottles after the Dreamkeeper, to be sure he'd stay away, but she knew it was too late. She knelt over Tristine's prone body. Her eyes staring up, unseeing, her skull caved in where the Dreamkeeper had struck her.

Cassidy kicked the Dreamkeeper's gun away with her foot and covered her face in her hands. She gave herself a moment before getting to her feet. The Dreamkeeper would be back, and she doubted he'd left her with the means to escape. For all of its outrageousness, this place did have the advantage of a quick lockdown. She grabbed as many bottles as she could fit into her pockets and wrapped Tristine's body in the Dreamkeeper's embroidered coat. Lifting the woman onto her shoulder, she took a look around the room. It glistened with shattered glass and glowed with dream dust, a small pool of blood on the floor where Merrick's aunt had died.

Returning the way she'd come, it came as little surprise that the tentacles were gone, unfurled and anchored somewhere below. A clever way to trap a thief. Cassidy placed Tristine's body gently against the wall and leaned out over an extended Dispensary tentacle, getting a sense of the dizzying height. She wouldn't survive a slide down something so vertical, not unless she had something to slow her descent. No, even then, she couldn't leave Merrick's aunt up here. She deserved better.

Cassidy moved to the rear of the room, throwing open the hatches. Maybe there was a building close by or a way to climb up to the balloon and fly the Dispensary elsewhere, touch down on some distant and teetering roof.

Flinging open the fourth hatch, a massive cephalopod's eyes stared in at her. Cassidy stumbled backward from the shock. "What do you want?" she shouted.

The Engineer continued to stare. Cassidy shook her head, venturing closer and gazing downward. The creature's tentacles led to the rooftop of a half-finished factory scraper. She couldn't jump it and survive, but... probably best not to think about it. Cassidy pulled Tristine's body onto her shoulder, hearing the clink of the dream dust bottles in her pockets. "If Gamgee could see me now," Cassidy said aloud.

With a whoop, she launched herself from the airship and onto the cool, clammy skin of the cephalopod's tentacle.

CHAPTER EIGHT

Gripping the tentacle between her thighs, Cassidy felt the cephalopod's lean muscles flex and rise at an angle, helping to slow her descent. The thick appendage thinned as she neared the bottom, the bulge of the suction cups on its underside rubbing over her knees. The beast was helping her, she knew, but some primal instinct made her physically recoil, even as the beast set her gently on the rooftop. Cassidy stared up into its squidgy face. "Thank you."

The Engineer blinked once and coiled its tentacle around Tristine's body. The Dreamkeeper's coat fell to the ground with a flash of red. The cephalopod lifted the body, staring at Tristine for a long moment before closing its eyes.

"No, don't go into hibernation mode again, I need that body back!" Cassidy shouted. "Her nephew deserves the chance to say goodbye."

The creature's eyelids did not move. "Give it back!" She reached inside her pocket for something to throw at the cephalopod, just hard enough to wake them up, get their attention, but all she could find were the bottles of dream dust. After staring at them, tempted, she shook her head and returned the bottles to her pockets. She couldn't squander something so precious to the dreamless.

Cassidy rifled through the pockets of the Dreamkeeper's coat. A ring of grime ran along the velvet inner collar, the edges beginning to fray. The pockets were worn smooth of their velvet and filled with the nonsense debris of a stranger's life: a pencil nub, a scuffed ring, a note written in an illegible hand. The coat's lining was a shiny black fabric, less obvious than a crimson coat on the arm of a woman walking through a sea of blue coveralls. Cassidy flipped it inside out, tucking the majority of the dream bottles she'd stolen into the pockets. She counted fourteen bottles before a sound from above startled her.

Shots skidded over the roof. Cassidy eyed the Dispensary overhead. The hatch hung open and the Dreamkeeper leaned out, sunlight glinting off of his gun. He must have been hiding up there the whole time. Cassidy wasted no time gathering the coat and escaping through the roof access.

Hugging the coat as she ran down the stairs, a waft of the Dreamkeeper's body odour rose from the lining. He must have worn the coat often. The stairway led on and on, as haphazardly added as the storeys themselves. In a place populated with the singular fashion of coveralls, citizens and Compliance Officers would know exactly where the coat had came from. She could ditch the thing, shove the bottles back into her coveralls, but she didn't.

Her knees grew wobbly as the floors gathered behind her, the echo of unseen machinery bouncing off metal handrails, odd smells growing, lingering, left behind for the next until at last the stairs ended and spilled her onto the now-familiar cobbled streets.

Ahead, a small group of red-headed women were being questioned by a Compliance Officer with a lean frame and a haircut Cassidy could only call a reverse pompadour. She held her breath and shifted down an alley adjacent to the building she'd left.

From the corner of her eye she saw a tentacle flash down from the Dispensary, likely depositing someone on the button to explain to Officer Pompadour how he'd lost their target. She ran, dodging into alleys until her way was barred by the gaping maw of an aqueduct over a dry riverbed.

A seething pile of textile factory trash, snippets of thread, broken bobbins and debris piled up in the riverbed. A lone woman, her hair tied up with a kerchief, used a pitchfork to pitch it all into the open aqueduct.

Cassidy plucked a piece of dark cloth from the pile and wrapped it over her hair to hide the red, wishing she hadn't stashed the abaya so far away. Grabbing a second pitchfork, she busied herself working alongside the woman, who gave her a nervous smile but said nothing. When Cassidy was finally convinced that neither the Dreamkeeper nor his Compliance Officers were following her, she thanked the woman and leaned the pitchfork back against the aqueduct wall, surprised to see a small crowd of dreamless appear in the gloom.

"Cassidy? What are you doing here?"

"Merrick?" She held out her hand to help him out of the garbage pit. "Running from Compliance Officers, of course. I was trying to infiltrate the Dispensary, what about you?"

Taking her hand, he stepped up beside her. His eyes were swollen, his nose running. "Looking for my aunt. Sometimes the dreamless come down here." He held out three coins. "I got my dream tokens and my work assignment. I can save her." His eyes glowed. "And since you know how the extraction went, maybe the Resistance has a better chance moving forward. Things are good."

"And I've got some dream dust for Minseo," she told him, showing him the bottles. She watched the sudden delight in his eyes as he recognized the coat, her heart sinking with the knowledge that delivering news of his aunt's death would destroy whatever victory they'd managed today.

"That's one for the books," he said, eyebrows high. "How did you steal the Dreamkeeper's jacket?"

Cassidy bit her lip. "He was beating a woman in the Dispensary, so I threw open bottles of dream dust at him and it got all over his coat. Apparently your Dreamkeeper has an imagination and didn't want to accidentally dose himself."

"He does. Dreamkeepers always do, it gives them the skills to put together dreams in new combinations." Merrick blew his nose into a handkerchief he pulled from his pocket. "Is the woman okay? Was she dreamless?"

Cassidy nodded. "Yeah." She took Merrick's hand and squeezed. "It was your aunt, Merrick. I'm so sorry, I couldn't stop him. She didn't make it."

Merrick stared at her, quiet, as her words sunk in. He dropped her hand and clenched his fists. "I had the tokens for her, why wouldn't she wait?"

"She was trying to steal dream dust, maybe for herself or for her friends down here. She grabbed a bottle and chugged it down before he got her."

"She did?" He tried to smile. "That's no small feat." He stared off into the darkness of the aqueduct. "Is she still up there?"

"No," answered Cassidy. "Believe it or not, one of the Engineers took her body."

"It did?" The sudden lightening of his tone was unmistakable. He swiped at the tears tracking down his cheeks. "It's considered a great honour to be laid to rest by the Engineers, but it hasn't happened in a long time."

"She must have been someone very special," said Cassidy.

Merrick held his face in his hands and stumbled slightly. "I feel terrible."

"That's understandable."

"I'm really sick. I need to lay down or I think I might fall."

"Okay, where can you do that? Would you like me to take you to Nightfall?"

"I got my barracks assignment this morning, it will be safe there," he said.

Cassidy thought of the building almost-collapse she'd witnessed earlier. "Merrick, do you know if anyone has ever been killed in a 'scraper collapse?"

"No, never. Why do you ask?"

"I think the Engineers are still watching out for you. They're not just sleeping."

Merrick shut his eyes and wobbled on his feet. "Sorry,

I'm having trouble keeping up with you. Everything feels so overwhelming."

"Let's get you home." Cassidy tightened the fabric hiding her hair and clutched the dreams again. "You'll have to direct me."

The barracks were a handful of residential high-rises clustered around the one that nearly collapsed earlier that day. The Engineers had drifted away. There remained an unmistakable purple haze to the structure. To Cassidy's chagrin, the damaged structure matched Merrick's assignment, some twenty flights up.

"Your world needs elevators, Mer," she muttered, waiting for him to stop and rest. Twenty flights of stairs were too much for someone as sick as he, but she doubted he'd appreciate it if she tossed him over her shoulder and marched him to his room. They made it eventually, the sway in the building knotting Cassidy's stomach.

His assignment was a tiny room with a bed, desk, lamp, and a single chair. He lay down on the bed with a small moan of comfort. She looked out a small window, sealed shut. The city sprawled along, the purple haze thin this time of day, the orange sky in strict contrast to the endless buildings.

"What do you think you're sick with?" she asked him.

"I don't know, I've never been sick like this before. My head is congested, my nose is stuffy, and my eyes feel hot."

Cassidy chuckled. "Sounds like you've got a man-cold."

"A what?"

"You know, a cold, but when a man has it." It felt like a jerk thing to say out loud. He shook his head and a shiver ran over Cassidy's spine. "A cold? It's a virus that affects your mucous membranes, causing congestion and a runny nose."

Merrick pulled the blanket over his body and shivered. "I've never heard of a virus like that before."

Cassidy sat down hard. No. No, no, no, that wasn't possible. Oh crap. Did she just bring her cold virus into a civilization with no immunity? Her heart sunk deep into her belly, remembering how such viruses had brought her world to a halt not so long ago.

CHAPTER NINE

Calm down, Cassidy told herself. Look at the facts. One individual sick, that's not a pandemic. Stay calm. But now she was inside a dormitory of people whom she'd just exposed to the virus, including everyone where she and Merrick had been since her arrival. There were at least a dozen dreamless in the bottom of Nightfall with them last night.

Cassidy reached for the bottles of dream dust. At least she could save them from one plague. She reached for an empty bottle from Merrick's desk, opened it, and poured the contents of the stolen bottles into it. When she wrapped the small bottles in the Dreamkeeper's coat again, the scuffed ring fell out of the pocket with a small tink of metal. Cassidy retrieved the ring and tucked it into her pants pocket beneath the coveralls. The bundled jacket and bottles she tucked under Merrick's bed.

His snores filled the room, no doubt worsened by his illness. Cassidy camped out in the chair, unwilling to leave him. Just because a virus is unknown doesn't mean it has to be deadly, she reminded herself, but that didn't make the hours pass by any quicker. She remembered now, too late, learning about dark tourism in her early anthropology courses; of the invisible diseases explorers spread to the people they met in their travels, decimating entire populations. She'd been a fool, gallivanting off to these uncharted worlds, never stopping to think what germs she might carry with her. Her thoughts filled with memories of the measures her world had to take when such virus' had happened there, and the fear and uncertainty that had followed. If Factorytown shut down like the countries of Earth did, how would anyone get their dreams? Her guts ached.

***

An alarm sounded throughout the building before dawn, startling Merrick awake. "Cassidy?" he sat up, groggy, his clothes crumpled and sweaty from fever.

"Yeah. Are you feeling any better?" The alarm went off again. "What is that?"

"Morning wake-up call, it's time for work." He threw his blanket off and struggled to his feet.

"Are you sure you're up for that?"

"No." He put his face into his hands. "I got assigned to work in the Dispensary. The place where she died, under the direct supervision of her murderer."

Cassidy's jaw dropped, her mind racing. "I'll go in your place. It's not safe; you said yourself that it's dangerous to be around the dream dust if you still have your imagination intact."

"The Dreamkeeper manages."

"Mer, let me go. Think about it: inside knowledge of

how the dream dust is made, how to fly the damn Dispensary, where it's stored. I could use this information to take them down. Imagine what this could do for the Resistance."

Merrick stared at her. "You're right."

"Perfect. Give me your identification or whatever, let me do this. I owe you in ways you don't know, please let me do this for you."

He shook his head. "You can't, Cassidy. He knows what you look like. They'll be looking for you. The Dreamkeeper isn't going to let you get away with stealing from him."

Cassidy blinked. The lack of sleep must be getting to her. He was right. "I don't want you near him, Merrick. He's dangerous and manipulative. He mesmerizes people, but none of it is real."

"I know," he said. "But I'm doing this. For my aunt, my parents, and everyone else."

The edge in his voice told Cassidy there was no stopping him. "Be careful," she said. "You caught this sickness from me and I am so sorry about that. It's annoying but relatively harmless back home but I can't say for sure that it will be the same here."

His eyes grew wide. "This could be bad, no?"

"I'll take care of you, I promise. This is my fault. For now, just listen: with this virus, sometimes you feel great in the morning, but symptoms come back." She reached for the cold pills she still had in her pocket. "These will help you stay alert if you need them. Don't let your guard down."

Merrick nodded. "And what are your plans for the

day, overthrowing the government?"

"Depends. Is there any chance of finding a coffee shop?"

"A what? I'm not sure what that is."

"I know. Don't worry about it." She followed him down the stairs, the bottle of dream dust tucked into her pocket, her red hair hidden inside the cloth again.

A man in a robot suit passed them by, taking the stairs two at a time. Merrick gestured to the dream dust with his hand. "Do you think you can save a little extra for Minseo?"

"Probably. How much do the dreamless need to give them a dream?"

"About a capful. Minseo would only need a fraction of that to run her tests."

The stairwell grew crowded with citizens leaving for work and the pair fell quiet, guarding their plans. Reaching the first floor, Merrick left the building alone while Cassidy held back to make sure they wouldn't be seen together. The steady stream of workers descending the stairs made her worry. She kept her gaze on the floor, a war waging in her conscience, sick with worry that she was exposing these people to a potentially dangerous virus while a bottle filled with life-saving dream dust waited in her pocket. Isolation and avoiding others had been key to surviving the plagues of her world, but the dust could only save lives if she gave it out. There was no obvious right or wrong path to take and it haunted her. She didn't know how the virus would affect anyone long term, but she did know that people were already dying from lack of dreams. *Act on the certainty, Cass,* she told herself.

She joined the flood outside the doors, keeping with the main flow of traffic until she passed a tight alley she could slip into unnoticed. The damp splash of small puddles between the cobbles gave a rhythm to her steps, the earthy smell reminding her of home with an unexpected pang of longing. She wondered how her family would fare in Factorytown. She hadn't seen anyone past middle age since she arrived. Her parents, like Merrick's, might have died of the plague years ago. She pushed the thought away, quickening her pace.

The alley opened up ahead and she stopped, gazing out carefully, tucking a few loose strands of telltale red into her makeshift kerchief. A lone woman sat in the middle of the square, sneezing and looking mystified by the action.

Cassidy's jaw clenched. Another person with a cold.

***

At last she arrived at Nightfall, ducking inside, hoping to find the Dreamless she'd seen there with Merrick two nights ago. Only two of the sickest among them remained, half-dead and unable to get to their feet, propped against the wall. One had a face so pale he looked blue, a dark hoodie pulled over his head, clutching the hand of a second person in a thick blue sweater, the blinking of their eyes the only indication they were alive.

"I have dreams for you," said Cassidy, falling to her knees before them and reaching into her pocket. When she withdrew the bottle the dust's blue glow chased away the shadows from their faces and their eyes locked on the dust in disbelief. "A capful, right?" She reached for the man's hand and shook as much into his hand. He held it to his friend's lips, who thanked Cassidy with their eyes.

"You, too," said Cassidy, shaking a second dose into his hand and watching him swallow it down. Then she closed his fist around the bottle. "I want you to take the rest and give it to anyone else who is dying. Can you do that?" He nodded. "Thank you. Now sleep, dream."

Cassidy left them to rest and climbed up Nightfall to find Minseo. Cassidy had retained a small bottle for the chemist, though a small part of her just wanted to see the girl to make certain she hadn't caught Cassidy's cold. Cassidy wasn't up for witnessing any deaths today, not from dreams, and definitely not from a freaking virus.

She tried to throw her frustration into the climb, but her fears were no stranger to adrenaline and followed her storey after storey. Had she saved the two Dreamless to watch them die of a cold instead? What about Merrick? Should she have quarantined him at home? Dammit. Gamgee should have sent an epidemiologist instead of her.

She was formulating a plan to take night classes in epidemiology when she reached HQ's window and slipped inside. "Minseo? Are you here?"

"Ah-choo!" was the only answer. Cassidy's hopes fell. "Minseo?"

"I'm here!" Cassidy pushed past the blackout curtain. Minseo sat at her desk, a small pile of tissues collecting at her side. "Cassidy, what brings you back here? Ugh, I'm sorry about this mess." She indicated the tissues. "I've got this virus that's been spreading around the city faster than Engineer fog. I've been watching it replicate here in the lab, and it's wild." She stopped, catching Cassidy's look. "Sorry, I didn't mean to bore you."

"It's not that. It's the virus—I'm worried it's my fault."

Minseo held a tissue to her nose and raised her eyebrows. "How could that be your fault?"

"It's a long story." Cassidy pulled out a small bottle. "I was able to get you some dream dust, though."

Minseo's eyes lit up. "Excellent!" She took the bottle from Cassidy and scooped a tiny measure into a glass tube that she slipped inside a magnification device with a click. Minseo blew her nose into a tissue before peering into her microscope. "Hmm. This is strange. The dust was physically changed since the last sample I received."

"Changed how?"

Minseo flipped slides, connected the microscope to a viewing device, and handed the device to Cassidy. "This is what the dust looked like on my last sample, and all samples before that, actually. See how it sits stationary in a crystalline structure on the slide?" She flicked to another slide. "This is what it looks like now. The crystalline structure is not just moving, it's dividing."

"What is this shadowy stuff attached to the crystal?" asked Cassidy.

"I'm not sure," said Minseo. "Oh, this is very exciting. I need to make some notes." She reached for a writing instrument but froze midway.

"Everything all right?"

Minseo sat back into her chair, her robot suit clinking against the metal frame. "That pattern of division is familiar." Her brow knitted lightly as she stared into space, a small blush creeping across her cheeks. "I saw this before. I saw it today." The crease between her eyes deepened for a moment before she leapt to her feet and flicked back several more slides, settling on a new one, with tiny blue globules shifting around the slide. "This is a cell sample I took from myself earlier today; watch the pattern of the division."

Cassidy straightened. "It's the same."

"Yeah. I fluoresced this sample and magnified it higher than the dust. I wonder what we'll see if I do the same with the dust." Minseo busied herself with the tools of her science, fingers moving with robotic reflexes faster than Cassidy could follow. Little time passed before the second sample was prepared and Minseo studied it through her lens.

"Is the shadowy stuff a virus parasite?"

"I think so," said Minseo. She tapped the device. "Look, you can see actually see the hole inside the crystal where the virus burrowed itself inside. This is impossible, this is a living parasite infecting what is essentially a solid object and giving it life. The Engineers must have something to do with this." Her voice trailed off, lost in her theories and calculations.

"So, my virus infected the dreams? What does that mean for people who need them?" It came out whinier than Cassidy would have liked, but her guts were sloshing with guilt and worry and oh god what had she just done to that poor couple at the bottom of Nightfall? She blanched. She'd handed them an entire bottle of dreams to give away, and she'd tossed the stuff all over the dispensary yesterday.

"I don't know," answered Minseo, her voice sounding far away. Cassidy may as well of not existed for how deep inside her thoughts she'd withdrawn. "But I'm going to find out."

"I'll see myself out," said Cassidy and headed for the ladder outside. Maybe the couple at the bottom of Night-fall were still asleep and she could get the bottle of dreams back from them: start there, worry about the Dispensary itself later. She needed to think. She needed a plan. She needed not to be the Typhoid Mary of this universe.

Her descent of Nightfall eschewed all local records, but it wasn't enough. The room where the two dreamless had slept was empty, nothing but the steady drip of moisture, the relentless clang of the nearby factories, and the endless purple fog to greet her.

Cassidy pounded her fists against the wall until she was spent and fell sagging to the floor, her head between her knees and her face hid from view.

CHAPTER TEN

"Cassidy! Wake up." Merrick's voice pierced through the fog of her sleep, his hand shaking her shoulder doing the rest.

She sat up and rubbed her eyes, disoriented in the gloom of the collapsed room. "Sorry. I didn't mean to fall asleep."

"I'm glad I found you. I'm on my lunch break." He chewed on the words like the phrase felt strange in his mouth. "There's a shipment of dream dust going to Shippingsburg this afternoon and I think I can get you on it. Compliance Officers are everywhere, Cass, and the Dreamkeeper has been threatening them that if they don't find you, he'll go after their dreams. You'd be safer in Shippingsburg." He smirked. "Unless you manage to anger their Dreamkeeper too."

Cassidy shook her head. "I can't, Merrick. I brought some dream dust to Minseo and she says the dust is infected with my cold virus."

Merrick sat down on his haunches beside her. "Almost the whole city is sick with it now. They had to shut down factories; I've never heard of that before."

Cassidy felt sick. This was like the plagues of her planet, all over again. "How are you feeling?"

"I felt pretty bad a few hours ago, but those pills you gave me worked wonders," he told her.

"That will only last a few hours. My god, Merrick, I'm so sorry. I never meant for this to happen."

"It's okay, Cassidy, honest. The Engineers won't let anything terrible happen to us." His eyes were full of concern.

God, he was a good kid. A swell of sisterly affection rose in Cassidy's chest. "The Engineers allowed the plague of the dreamless to happen, Mer; forgive me if I don't trust them to stop another."

He dropped his gaze. "I guess, but you can't just give up and hide out in this broken basement. Do something."

Cassidy's pride burned at the idea that she needed to hear those words, but here she was. "Yeah, but do what?" She thought over what he had said about the shipment. "The dust on the new shipment is probably contaminated, which means we can't send it to Shippingsburg. Maybe if we're lucky, we can contain the outbreak to Factorytown. You said you could get me onto the shipment?"

He nodded, looking unsure now.

She licked her lips, a plan forming. "How many guards are on a ship?"

"None, just the pilot. It takes imagination to plan a heist, and as far as they know, nobody here has one but kids."

Cassidy smiled. "Except for us."

"Come on, then." Merrick reached for her hand and got to his feet. "I've spent the morning training in the shipping department. It's not on the Dispensary ship, but it is at the top of the building where we met."

It would be some relief to find the building with the portal home again, if she didn't accidentally wipe out this population first. "Is the extraction device still broken?"

"Yeah." He grinned. "Come on, the cargo ship is sitting in the warehouse dock, getting loaded."

Cassidy scrambled to her feet, her calf muscles stiff from Factorytown's stairs. "So different cities share dream dust?"

"It was news to me too. I guess the CEOs trade them."

"I take it Shippingsburg is owned by a different CEO, then?"

"Exactly. My trainer's been trying to explain it to me, but it doesn't make any sense. Doesn't Shippingsburg have their own Engineers?"

"Wait, you're saying the dream dust is traded like a commodity?" She waited for Merrick's nod. "No wonder the Dreamkeeper won't give the dreamless any for free, it's what is making the CEOs rich." At the least the virus she'd brought into this world was accidental; these monsters were intentionally letting people die of the plague to make money.

She kept her makeshift kerchief tight over her hair and her head low as Merrick led her through the maze of Factorytown and into the high-rise where they'd met. Cassidy groaned internally at the idea of another dizzying staircase. "Does the Dreamkeeper have his own elevator or does he take the stairs like everyone else?"

"Apparently, the Dispensary ship drops him off at his penthouse apartment before it docks at the warehouse for the night."

Cassidy slowed her pace on the stairs. "This airship hijacking, can it be tied back to you?"

"Nah, I'm the new guy. I can't even drive the things yet."

Cassidy swallowed back a statement that she couldn't fly one either. She'd figure it out. "Here's my plan: I can't risk infecting another city, and I know this dream dust has been contaminated with my virus. Instead of taking it to Shippingsburg, I'm going to unload it into Nightfall. There's plenty of room in there, and Minseo can study it to her heart's content. If somehow it ends up being safe, we can distribute it freely to everyone in Factorytown from there. But first we need to make sure the Dispensary doesn't come anywhere near Nightfall until I'm gone."

Merrick's expression cheered. "One of the Dispensary pilots is a Resistance member, he could help."

She put her hand on his arm. "Is there any way you could be there too, just in case something comes up that needs some creative problem solving, like a lie? It'll take an imagination to think fast in that situation."

"I still have my tokens. I could duck out of the warehouse early and head to the Dispensary, pretend I'm shopping for my first dream."

"Good, that'll work," said Cassidy, thinking quickly. Everything was falling into place, so long as she could figure out the airship.

"How do we get rid of the cargo pilot?"

Cassidy shrugged. "We'll figure that out when we get up these damn stairs. Factorytown citizens must have calves of steel." She fell silent, thinking, her head full of problems needing solving. She knew from experience that worrying about them wouldn't do any good, their solutions would come when their full details were fleshed out in the moment, but Merrick was with her and the fun of risk was dampened significantly by the thought of something bad happening to him. Even now he wheezed slightly, working away at the stairs, the symptoms of his cold breaking through despite the medication.

Sweat trickled freely down her back before they reached the warehouse at the top of the skyscraper, the sway in the building giving Cassidy the sensation of mild seasickness. It was hard to forget that these buildings had an unsettling tendency to collapse. She'd be happy to climb aboard the airship she couldn't fly and leave it behind.

Merrick pushed open a door atop the final staircase, the sound echoing downward behind them and forward through the shining, vast, and empty room. If dream dust was indeed a commodity, it was either all inside the ship already, or Bezanson was broke. Either way, he was about to be once she had the dust in her hands. Her resolve strengthened, worry giving way to the clear, clean mental precision of her beloved adrenaline, her pulse climbing quickly higher in her fingertips.

Stepping out into the smoggy orange air of an outdoor hangar, Cassidy caught her first glimpse of a cargo ship. Unlike the cephalopod-shaped balloon of the Dispensary, this looked like an Earth Zeppelin, complete with a vast gas envelope hugging a long shipping container below its belly. A walkway and safety rails lined the container's roof, an engine room sitting tidily up front and four strong, pivoting propellers below that, protected by a series of steel cages attached to the container itself.

Merrick strolled over to a group of workers standing around, their work complete, waiting for the ship to take off. Cassidy ducked along the far side of the dock, waiting until she was out of sight to jump up and grab hold of the container's upper safety rail. Pulling herself onto the ship, she found a clear line of sight into the engine room, with no pilot present. Peering back towards Merrick, she saw a woman with a headset chatting with the group. Cassidy shrugged; couldn't beat that kind of easy.

She turned to the airship's controls, a mess of toggle switches, dials, and levers. The symbols were unfamiliar and non-intuitive. Did the damn thing have any pedals like a proper plane? She checked; it did. Pulling the chair closer, she pressed a pedal cautiously and the airship started to rise, slowly at first, then faster, ropes skittering off the ship as the shouts of the pilot and warehouse crew fell behind her.

Her sense of victory faded as a maze of skyscrapers she'd have to manoeuvre through loomed ahead. Cassidy swallowed hard, flicking each toggle and dial, trying to determine which one controlled the propellers she'd seen below so she could steer the damn ship. She depressed the only button on the beast and a half-moon steering wheel popped up from a compartment amid the toggles.

"How is that efficient?" she muttered in disgust, clutching the wheel with both hands and working to get a feel for piloting the zeppelin. Now all she had to do was find Nightfall.

Her breath calmed for the first time that day; the view beyond the airship too stunning to ignore, dark monoliths piercing an orange sky with layers of smog and purple haze. Here and there a cephalopod hung stark in the distance, lending the landscape such an otherworldly vibe that she fumbled for her phone again, taking one more photo. Hopefully it would remind her of something more than killing a dimension of humanoids. Hopefully, she still had a chance to redeem herself here.

CHAPTER ELEVEN

Cassidy flew the airship low and slow, keeping close to the worker's barracks and an eye out for the Dispensary. Finally, she lowered the airship onto Nightfall, the caged propellers striking the broken skyscraper rougher than she would have liked, shaking a few bricks loose in the crumbling sections leaning against the nearby buildings.

After several minutes of attempting to shut the ship down, she gave up and left it idling as she lowered herself into the cargo hold and pushed open the big bay doors. Inside lay half a palette of dream dust in cloth sacks. Cassidy stared at it, questioning. Only half a palette? As commodities went, that was very little dust. Compared to Earth, she reminded herself. Comparisons need not apply on a strange world in a strange dimension. Still, an entire airship to ship a cargo so small seemed like overkill. Surely a smaller ship would have been more efficient, unless the show of pomp mattered more than the actual dust.

Cassidy shook her head and hoisted a sack onto her shoulder, carrying it out of the airship and tossing it gently into a vacant room on the other side of a window several stories short of Minseo and HQ. If by chance she was seen, she'd prefer not to incriminate them. Scanning the sky, she saw nothing out of the ordinary, just buildings and orange. She ducked inside the hold and hoisted two sacks this time, testing the weight and finding her footing secure. This time, when she stepped out into the daylight, her view was blocked by a sudden quartet of Engineers closing in around her. Cassidy's first instinct was one of fright, but when she pushed past her fear she realized the cephalopods had significantly concealed her from the sight of any airships which might happen upon them.

She nodded at them from between the sacks of dust on either shoulder. "Thanks." The creatures did not respond, but she liked it best that way and carried on her work. Her half palette she estimated to hold untold thousands worth of dreams, but they fit into a mere twenty-one sacks. She finished shifting the dust in a lather, small bits of glowing dust clinging to her sweaty skin where it had seeped through the weave of the sacks. She'd take her chances with what small danger that might put her in, she decided, certain it was less than she'd thrown at the Dreamkeeper in the Dispensary.

When she returned to the airship's engine room, the Engineers drifted quietly away, their tentacles shifting slightly and their bodies gliding through the air like water.

The air ship followed them with significantly less grace, Cassidy eager to put some distance between herself and Nightfall but unsure of her next move. The ship wasn't something she could park and hope it went unnoticed. She couldn't return it to the dock where surely Compliance Officers would be waiting. She rose above the 'scrapers, looking down over the city for somewhere to park the beast, her breath catching to see how it sprawled on and on and on, in every direction, without breaking.

In the far distance, a half-heartedly built wall wove in and out of the taller buildings, giving Cassidy the distinct impression that this was the border of Factorytown. The humanoids had used up every available space and had started climbing into the cephalopod's sky. Cassidy wondered how the cephs felt about that, and if this was something that they could have suspected when they brought the humans to this place. But then again, looking up into the unfathomable free space above it all, maybe this was nothing to them.

The fuel gauges on the zeppelin still read half full, so she pushed the throttle forward, making slow progress. She supposed a big enough roof would work, though all the stacked factories below appeared too rickety to handle much extra weight. Turning the ship carefully around, it puttered in the opposite direction as three birds rose to join her on the horizon.

The orange of the sky deepened, warning Cassidy that she had little time to find a safe place to land and somewhere to spend the night before the grid shut everything into darkness. She squinted downwards, half her mind on the horizon and the other half searching for a decent structure. Another fallen scraper, far from Nightfall, would work.

A new engine joined the sound of the zeppelin, setting Cassidy at full attention, throbs of adrenaline pulsing in her ears. The birds were much larger. "Crud, those aren't birds," she said aloud. "Crap, Cass. You need to pay more attention, you haven't seen a damn bird since you popped into this world."

Smaller airships, clearly built for speed and manoeuvrability, no doubt belonging to the Compliance Officers, zoomed towards her. She wasn't going to be able to outrun them in this monstrous rig, but she might be able to lose them long enough to land the beast and make a run for it. Steering downward, into the thick of the skyscraper forest where it was already getting dark, she manoeuvred her ship past emptying factories, their constant spew of exhaust easing, making it easier to see but also to be seen.

A sharp metallic clink rang sudden in Cassidy's ears: bullets ricocheting off the container beneath her. Dang it. One wrong spark and the gas bag above her head would ignite and she'd Hindenburg all over Factorytown, sending a heavy metal box careening down on top of who knows how many innocent people. Cassidy set her jaw, furious and refusing to allow any of it to happen.

Steering the ship dangerously low, she skimmed along the second stories of the factories, tornadoes of purple fog swirling away from her propellers. At least down here the container wouldn't have far to fall, and the streets were emptying fast, escaping the approaching dark. Cassidy tapped the controls with her fingers. She didn't want to get stuck down here in the thick dark of a Factorytown night either, bump steering off of rickety skyscrapers.

She had no choice but to go higher and find somewhere safe to land, hunching her head as more bullets clinked against the ship. The Dreamkeeper obviously didn't want his ship back, she decided, throwing whatever caution Cassidy Cane was capable of to the winds and pushing the throttle full bore, yanking the kerchief from her hair, stuffing it into her pocket and shaking her red hair into the wind.

A large cephalopod floated ahead. She flinched as the whiz of a bullet left a breath of wind on her cheek, hoping the officers wouldn't shoot at the Engineers, but neither trusting them not to. Banking left around a leaning 'scraper, she bypassed the cephalopod before it came within shooting range of the idiots tailing her, only to find another pair of cephalopods dead ahead. She swore under her breath, banking right this time, squinting to see by the meagre lights of the factories as the last light of the sun winked out. The cephalopods were only shadows in the distance now as her hand automatically slowed the ship to a crawl and the grid went off with a hush, leaving her in darkness.

Her breath and the sound of the zeppelin's engines seemed the only thing that existed in the universe. She closed the throttle, feeling the airship lurch. Her mind searched for her next move while her fingers probed the controls, forcing herself to remember where everything was located. Her foot tapped on the pedals. Those, at least, were easy.

Her only reassurance was the knowledge that the ships giving chase were in the same situation. Did she wait here, in stasis, until the ship ran out of fuel? She was kilometres above the ground; she'd never survive the fall. Her mind groped for the next solution. Every problem solved as it came, in order, no hesitation. That is how to survive. First problem: she needed light. She hunted through her pockets. A forgotten bottle of dream dust, the Dreamkeeper's scuffed ring, her pocketknife, and a bit of paper, the nonsense scribbles from the crimson coat. Could she use the pocketknife and the ring to create some sort of spark and ignite the paper? Maybe, if the paper only needed to burn for a minute or less. Crud. She was in some real trouble here. Wait, the dust. It had glowed before. She shook the bottle, the blue glow of the dust igniting, bright enough to see the controls of the airship. It wasn't much, but it was a start.

Cassidy held up the bottle, hoping it might reflect off the windows of the nearby buildings, giving her something to steer by. Instead, a soft rose light responded to the dreams, growing brighter, longer, rippling. Another light rose to her left, and another. Cassidy watched in awe as the light grew strong enough to frame the cephalopod tentacles it was fluorescing from. "Phosphorescence, that's amazing," said Cassidy under her breath, kicking the zeppelin into action again.

But if she had enough light to fly by, so did the Compliance Officers. Rounding another building, a smattering of cephalopods in the distance lit up in response to the others. Cassidy couldn't help but smile, until one of the small black ships pulled into position in front of her, close enough for Cassidy to spit on.

The pilot got to his feet, standing tall and bathed in the Engineers' glow: the Dreamkeeper himself. A sneer split his face and he fell into a dramatic bow before raising his gun and aiming it at Cassidy's head. "You have something that belongs to me!" he hollered over the roar of the engines.

He seemed to expect an answer before he fired his weapon, but Cassidy wasn't interesting in playing his game. She pushed the throttle hard and fast, ramming the small ship, sending the Dreamkeeper off his feet, and the ship scuttling downward.

The ships behind her opened fire, whatever they'd been holding back before abandoned as they saw the Dream-keeper's ship fall. The soft light of the cephalopods' phosphorescence was broken by a thick sheet of sparks flying behind the bullets as Cassidy steered the ship in a zigzag pattern, knowing she was running out of time and ideas.

A cephalopod in her path moved suddenly toward her. "No, no," cursed Cassidy, "I need you to get out of my way."

A whoosh of heat and the world around her erupted in fire, the force of her ship's gas envelope igniting throwing her from her feet. She closed her eyes as something squeezed around her waist and drew her from the heat and into the cool, sweet air beyond.

CHAPTER TWELVE

Cassidy forced herself to smile at the cephalopod who had rescued her, unnerved by the squeeze of its tentacle around her waist. The creature had another tentacle wrapped around the container pod of her wrecked ship. She breathed a small sigh of relief that it wouldn't be crashing down atop of anyone.

The cephalopod pulled her, still coiled in their limb, up to their face. "Hello human," the creature spoke into her mind, its face never moving save a slow and steady blinking. "We sense you are afraid of us."

"Yeah, well, you're very large and I don't fully understand what your relationship with the local humans is," Cassidy said aloud, hoping the ceph would understand.

"Then I will tell you," said the cephalopod, its voice shifting to more soothing tones. "When we first encountered humanoids, the presence of imagination in their brainwaves gave us a wonderful gift, and my people dreamed for the first time. These dreams pushed out our stress and our worries for a short time, and we delighted in them. When we learned the human colony was adrift without a home, we invited them to join us here on our world. The resources the humans needed to live did not overlap with our needs and their population's imaginations granted us our dreaming."

Cassidy closed her eyes, trying to make sense of the mismatched pieces of information she'd gleaned from this strange world. "Then why are you collecting their imaginations to make new technologies?"

The massive eyes wobbled with reflections of wavering phosphorescence as a great tear gathered. "We have never done what we stand accused of."

"Okay," said Cassidy, worried the creature's massive tear might flood the street below. "I believe you, but I don't understand."

"Before the human colonies arrived here, the humans sent five engineers to create the human cities to house them. One of these engineers, Dr. Chimi, became a great friend to my people. It was she who first discovered that she could use our night fog in combination with human engineering to manufacture human food and materials. She shared her discovery with the other engineers and prepared for the arrival of their families. Many times the other engineers wanted to set up an economic system, but Dr. Chimi thought it best to keep all humans equal. For many years the human lived peacefully, the original engineers held in high esteem and seen as leaders."

"As they aged, Dr. Chimi's wife fell ill with a rare disease that removed her ability to differentiate between reality and fantasy. They came to us for help. Together, we determined that if we removed Tarryn Chimi's imagination, her life could be spared. Dr. Chimi knew her beloved would not be able to dream properly following the extraction of her imagination, so she found a way to turn the imagination into a dream dust that could be administered over her wife's lifetime."

Cassidy's heart sank. "Oh, no." A breeze blew up from the city below, its skyline a soft silhouette in the glow of cephalopod phosphorescence, but that wasn't what made her shiver.

"The other engineers had grown jealous of Chimi's success. They wanted her inventions under their own control, and in her Imagination Extraction Device they saw a terrible potential. When Dr. Chimi refused to turn over the device for widespread usage, the engineers murdered the Chimis, copied the device, and split the human civilization amongst themselves. When the humans resisted, the engineers told them that the directive to remove their imaginations came from us, that we now required their imaginations to make the technologies that made our world habitable for humans. We did not discover this until it was far too late."

"Why didn't you tell the humans the truth?"

The cephalopod closed its eyes a moment, its own glow dimming below. Cassidy glanced downward when she noticed, awarded with a strange view of sleek tentacles shivering into darkness below.

"We were too late. Our brains are well suited to long, deep ruminations, rather than the quick wit and reflex of a human. We discovered that our communication with humans requires both an intact and fully matured brain. By the time we knew to speak up, the only humans left who could understand us were also the ones responsible for our silence."

Cassidy wondered if the engineers knew that or if they'd gotten lucky with a side effect they didn't know to look for. She had a hunch it was the former. "You could have destroyed the IEDs."

"We considered this, but we feared that without a renewing source of dream dust, the CEOs would hoard what remained and the humans would die in horrific numbers. Instead, we formed a new plan. We dug wormholes and placed portals in other human worlds, leaving members of our kind as sentinel within them, and waited. Now, here you are."

"But it's been *generations* of suffering. You helped create that device; you have some responsibility here. Maybe you prefer meditation or whatever, but you're capable of saving entire buildings from collapse; you need to step up and help these people. They are broken, yet they still look up to you."

"You are here now."

"Yeah, and I brought a virus with me that's causing a pandemic. Can you do anything about that?"

"We are aware of your virus," said the cephalopod.

"You knew?" Cassidy asked. "Do you have any idea how dangerous this is? My friend down there is sick, and I may have infected the entire city with a novel virus. I've seen this happen on my own world; a lot of people died. *A lot.*"

"We altered the virus to our will when we reconfigured the language centre of your brain. The virus will not cause lasting harm."

Cassidy rubbed her forehead. "What are you talking

about?"

"Before we allowed you to enter our world, we altered your brain to act as a universal translator. Without it you would not be able to understand the human's dialect nor ours."

She remembered the cephalopods inside the portal, both the discomfort and the personal invasion of the tentacle that probed her mouth and ears. "That was... brain surgery?"

"Yes. We altered you to give you the ability to understand and speak all languages you may encounter. It is both a skill needed to serve our purpose and a gift for your efforts."

She was speechless. On the one hand, she was furious that her consent had not been obtained before messing around in her brain, but on the other, she'd been given an incredible gift. More importantly, the cephalopod said no harm would come from her virus. The cephs had saved the people in the collapsing building; Cassidy knew they had the human's best interests at heart. Her shoulders sagged with relief. Maybe she hadn't killed everyone after all.

"Will you speak to the humans for us and tell them the truth of their stolen imaginations?" asked the cephalopod.

"I will." She furrowed her brow, thinking. "You said human imaginations helped you dream. Does that mean you haven't been dreaming either?"

"We have not."

She nodded. "Then, if it comes to it, you'll help the citizens fight the CEOs?"

"We will." Its tentacles wiggled with seeming discomfort. "Though we may need direction to act as quickly as the humans."

"Okay, I can do that." Cassidy took a deep breath. All she had to do was to stage a coup, no big deal. She stared over the city, dark and alien with glowing tentacles spaced out across the horizon, whatever stars shone above cloaked behind thick and smoggy clouds. Her misgivings faded into a giddy sense of abandon. Why the heck not add coup to her growing resume, after all?

"We will take you to your friend Merrick, if you would like," the cephalopod offered.

Her giddiness faded, replaced with worry. She hoped her friend was okay. "I'd appreciate that."

The cephalopod placed the container it was still holding gently atop a nearby building as the group of cephalopods' glowing phosphorescence faded and went out. The tentacle around Cassidy's waist was reassuring in the dark as air moved against her skin, but she saw nothing of their journey. Her feet touched ground and the tentacle loosened gently from her waist, leaving her unanchored in the darkness.

CHAPTER THIRTEEN

Cassidy reached for the bottle of dream dust in her pocket and shook it alight. "Merrick?" The blue in the bottle shimmered and grew stronger. Cassidy expected to find herself in Merrick's barrack, but instead it was a much larger space with half a dozen wide-eyed faces looking her way.

"Cassidy? Where did you come from?" It was Merrick's voice. "It's all right, everybody, she's one of us."

Someone lit a lantern, a strange-looking contraption Cassidy had no doubt ran on cephalopod fog. Another lantern lit up, and another, faces unfamiliar until she met Minseo's eyes. "Merrick called an emergency meeting of the Resistance," she said.

"At first it was to find out what happened to you," Merrick told her. "But you need to hear this. Paul?"

A man in a hoodie with a long face stepped into the light. Cassidy recognized him as one of the two Dreamless she'd given dust to earlier that day. The change in him was tremendous; his eyes twinkled, his skin vibrant.

"The dream dust you gave me this morning restored

my imagination. I can imagine again, great epic flights of fancy, stories of things I've never seen, people I've never met. It's wonderful! And it's the same with my friend, the one who took the dust with me."

"The same happened to me," said a woman Cassidy didn't recognize. "Except I got my dust from the Dispensary."

"We think that somehow the virus-infected dream dust is regenerating people's imaginations," said Minseo, clasping her hands to contain her glee.

Cassidy chuckled. "That's what the cephalopods meant." Met with a dozen puzzled glances, she went on. "They told me that they altered the virus, though I didn't understand how."

"You're saying the Engineers are awake? They're speaking to you?" Merrick's eyes were wide.

"Yes, they are, they did, and they want you to know that they never wanted your imaginations. The extractions had nothing to do with them, it was all the CEOs. Apparently, you need to have an un-extracted, mature brain to be able to understand the cephalopods. Once you lost your imaginations, they couldn't communicate with you anymore, so they couldn't tell you themselves."

The rebels exchanged glances, their expressions a gallery of confusion. Paul spoke first. "If our imaginations weren't extracted for the Engineers, why do the CEOs want it?" His voice sounded tight, his fists clenched at his sides.

"Has anyone here actually seen any new tech in the past decade?" asked Merrick, his tone quiet. "Or have we always been too poor, too focused on getting that next dream, to see it?"

"The CEOs have been extracting your imaginations to make you dependent on dream dust. It allows them to control you and brings them unlimited wealth and power." Cassidy took a deep breath. This wouldn't be easy for them to hear. "The dream dust is made from your extracted imaginations. The CEOs are taking it out of you to sell it back to you."

No one said anything for a long moment. A sob rose from the rebels. "Monsters," whispered someone.

Merrick met Cassidy's eyes and nodded, stepping forward and taking one of the lanterns. Holding it up high, he looked into the eyes of everyone in the room one at a time before he spoke. "What they did to us is terrible and we have every right to be angry and rage over the loved ones that we have lost to this unthinkable greed, and we will, but right now we have a chance to change everything. We have a virus that can restore to us the very power they stole. Now is not the time to withdraw and come to terms with what has happened, now is the time to get out there and get this infected dust into every citizen of Factorytown who has been wronged."

The energy in the room shifted as his words ignited a spark in the darkness. His listeners stood taller, their shoulders straightened, jaws firm.

"We take back what they have stolen and we destroy the means to take it again," he told them.

"How are we going to get dust to everyone who needs it?" asked Paul.

Merrick gestured to Cassidy with the lantern. "Cassidy stole a shipment of dream dust this afternoon; we'll start with that."

The expressions that turned to her now were ones of surprise and respect. "I stashed the stolen dust in Nightfall, just a few storeys down from HQ," she told them.

Minseo gave her an odd look. "We're in HQ right now."

Cassidy considered explaining how she'd travelled by a cephalopod to get here, and apparently magicked through a wall, but thought better of it. They'd had enough shocks for one evening. "Will there be enough dust in there for everyone?" she asked Merrick.

"Probably not," he said, "but it would have to be close."

"It's possible that since the virus is restoring the imagination, we may be able to give a smaller dose," said Minseo. "I could run some tests, figure out the best dose with minimal waste. I'll need a few volunteers, but the only side effect would be an imagination. We'd best get started right away."

"I'll volunteer," a few people spoke up at once.

Merrick nodded. Cassidy watched him from afar, wondering when he'd become the leader of the Resistance. The others seemed happy to defer to him, but she had a strange sad feeling like he'd just grown up in front of her.

The group fell into a murmur, small conversations working out different methods of transferring dust over the town, how to ensure no one was missed, and staying hidden from Compliance Officers.

"There's plenty more dust in the Dispensary," said Cassidy, loud enough to make sure she'd been heard. Merrick levelled his gaze at her and nodded. "I'll go with you."

"So will I," said Paul.

"I'll come too," said a woman wearing a kerchief over her dark hair. Cassidy recognized her as the woman who'd been pitching trash into the aqueduct yesterday. "I'm Esmerelda."

Cassidy gave her a warm smile. "Esmerelda, I want you dosed before we go. If we get into trouble, we'll need creative problem-solving and heaps of lying, so let's make sure we have the best advantage of that. Merrick, what are the odds the Dreamkeeper actually parked the Dispensary at the warehouse after it was robbed?"

Merrick shook his head. "I don't know, but I do know they set up guards to watch the warehouse overnight. They were buzzing around in small black ships when I left."

Cassidy knew just what ships he meant. "Oh good, maybe we can hijack one. Can anyone fly those things?"

"I used to pilot the Dispensary before I got sick," said Paul.

Cassidy eyed him with a new respect. "The Dreamkeeper didn't provide his own Dispensary staff with dreams to keep them from stealing?"

"No," said Paul, crossing his arms. "He used fear instead."

"His wife was actually one of us," said Merrick quietly. "She's the one who smuggled dream dust out for Minseo for study. I'm worried he found out and did something terrible to her."

Cassidy pulled her hair back into a tight ponytail. "We might find her yet, Mer, but we've got to make it to the Dispensary before daybreak if we want to steal that dust."

Paul held back, reaching for one of the fog-powered lanterns. The light was dim and Cassidy wondered how they were all going to scale down Nightfall safely, but Paul led the quartet through a hatch in the makeshift floor instead, sliding along the tilted floor until they reached a window at the bottom of the building. He flipped it open, reached for a length of rope attached to a heavy beam nearby, and threw it down.

"This way is safer after dark," Merrick told her, catching her eye. Reaching for a metal figure eight hanging on a nail, he wrapped the rope around it. "I'll go first." Holding on to the eight, he jumped through the window, the rope hissing the long way to the ground.

Paul and Esmerelda pulled the rope back, retrieving the figure eight and releasing the rope again. Esmerelda wrapped the rope around the eight a second time. "You hold on here and here," she showed Cassidy. "Would you like to go this time?"

"Sure, I love zip lining into certain doom." She regretted her snark when she noticed Esmerelda's surprised look. "Sorry, my sense of humour is an acquired taste. I'll go." She grabbed the device as she'd been directed and stepped through the window.

The hiss of the rope against the metal filled her ears, pushing out her other senses even as they desperately probed the humid, inky darkness for clues. The acrid smell of the city eased this late at night, the smog rising away or swept along by a breath of wind winding through the cobblestoned streets, giants hushing in the darkness overhead. Instead, a smell of mildew and warm stone hung in the air, with the soft and ever-present ocean smell she'd come to associate with the cephalo-fog.

Cassidy jerked to a stop. She fumbled with the device in her hands to no avail. She listened, hearing not a single breath in the pitch black of the night. Cassidy swung her feet, stretching, but touched nothing. Was she close to the ground? She felt for the rope with her feet, finding nothing. Next, with one hand, finding the end of the rope in a knot just past her figure-eight. Where the hell was Merrick? Had he fallen to his death? "Dammit," she cursed, furious.

"Cassidy?" It was Merrick's voice. "The rope's a few feet short; you'll have to drop the rest of the way, but—"

Cassidy let go, tucking in and ready to roll if she needed to, but she landed well. "Got it. Could have warned me about the rope, though."

"If I'd known about it, I would have," said Merrick, his voice magnified in the darkness.

Cassidy wanted to scold him for jumping without knowing, but she bit her tongue; she'd been about to do the same. Esmerelda came next, then Paul with the lantern.

They crept along the dark street, the soft light of the lantern little more than a single Christmas light against the dark. Alone she would have been helplessly lost, but the others knew the streets of Factorytown well and guided their small group from one block to the next, until they reached an all too familiar stairwell and Cassidy's calves reminded her how long it had been since she'd had a good sleep.

When the group reached the warehouse and peered outside to the docking structure, the Dispensary was not there. "Where else could it be?" asked Esmerelda.

A lump of crimson fabric in the centre of the warehouse caught Cassidy's eye. She left the group, walking over to it, hoping she was wrong. The texture of velvet brushed against her fingertips, the familiar weight heavy in her hands. She opened it to be sure, hiding it from the others' view with her body: the Dreamkeeper's jacket she'd stolen from the Dispensary. She rubbed her thumb over the stained velvet. Cassidy had left the jacket rolled and stowed beneath Merrick's bed. The Dreamkeeper must have discovered Merrick's role in all of this. A chill ran over her skin.

CHAPTER FOURTEEN

"Cassidy?" asked Merrick. "Where should we go next?"

She rolled up the coat. "The Dreamkeeper's house. Paul, can you get us there?"

He held up his hands in apology. "I've only ever gone there by ship."

"Then we go by ship," said Cassidy, flinging open the doors and stepping out into the open.

"Cassidy, wait! There are Compliance Officers out there!"

"That's what I'm counting on," she said, never breaking her gaze into the darkness.

The sound of engines firing up and the click of the dock's spotlights coming on, aiming for her eyes, sent her pulse to ecstatic levels. Oh yes, she had been getting a little stale, hadn't she? She couldn't see, but she recognized the engine sound of the bird ship that had chased her earlier that night. There was at least one still intact, and if she was correct, the pilot would be under orders to find her and come in for a closer look.

Cassidy held back against the now-closed doors, making the officers come past the spotlights if they wanted to be sure in their reports to the Dreamkeeper. After a long moment, the ship moved ahead. She waited. A little closer and she could almost see the officer's face. He moved forward again, leaning ahead, close enough that she could see him squint. Now. She charged toward him, legs pumping. He wouldn't be able to shift the ship around in such a tight space before she reached him. Reaching for the railing around his cockpit, Cassidy swung herself into the small gondola, the ship rocking as the bird-shaped gas balloon above worked to balance out the sudden weight.

"Hi!" she said to the pilot, pulling back and punching him in the jaw. Her knuckles erupted with fire, but the pilot didn't go down. Grabbing him around the back, she brought up her knee at the same time she pushed him into it, knocking the wind from his lungs. As he gasped for air, she made short work of tying his hands behind his back.

She gestured to the others to come outside and climb aboard as she hauled the Compliance Officer into the warehouse.

"You don't have to be so rough," said the officer. "I get assigned my job the same as everyone," he muttered.

Cassidy stopped. She hadn't considered that. "Do you have an imagination?"

"No, of course not."

Cassidy gave him a crooked grin and pulled the bottle of dream dust from her pocket. She pinched a bit between her fingers. "Open up." The officer complied and she sprinkled it on his tongue. "Long story short: it's the CEOs who take your imaginations to sell them back to you. This dose is going to give you your imagination back, so don't squander it and maybe look the other way if you see anyone giving it out, okay?"

The shock on his face could not have been faked. Cassidy nodded and turned to go. "I hate to leave you like this but I can't have you squealing until you believe me, so have a good night, I guess." She swung out the door and ran to the ship where Paul was already taking control, rising from the dock. Merrick and Esmerelda had pulled one of the spotlights onto the ship for light.

Cassidy looked on, marvelling. "All this cool tech, but no one thought of headlights?"

Esmerelda shook her head. "The Engineers need the darkness for their courtship rituals, it was part of the agreements when we were allowed to populate this planet."

Merrick chuckled. "I never knew that, that's kind of..." his face fell into an uncomfortable grimace and suddenly he looked sixteen again.

Cassidy laughed. "Well, here's hoping we don't accidentally peep on any mating cephalopods."

The ship banked heavily around a building and hovered before a glass house built into the side of a high-rise. Not a clever penthouse, but certainly Factorytown's brand of risky architecture. To its side, tucked into scaffolding, waited the Dispensary.

The spotlight reflected back from the Dreamkeeper's glassy walls like a myriad of shattered diamonds. Staring at the building with her jaw clenched, Cassidy slipped her arms into the Dreamkeeper's coat to keep her arms free and ready to fight if need be. Ink stains at the bottom of the right cuff caught her eye and she turned her palm up to see them better. The fabric showed extra wearing there. She looked up, catching Merrick's questioning expression and shrugging in response.

Pulling alongside the Dispensary, Esmerelda, Cassidy, and Merrick, holding the lantern, leapt from the small ship onto the upper deck of the Dispensary. A vast burner and gas tubes took up most of the surface space, with a small railing encircling the area and probably the best view in the city when the sun was high. The hatch in the floor leading to the Dispensary was locked.

Cassidy leaned over the railing, spying a window below. Pulling out her pocketknife, she opened it and slammed the point into the glass. As she pulled her arm back, the window shattered, tinkling to the deck below. She grinned at Merrick and swung herself into the window, unlocked the hatch from within, and let the others inside.

Creeping through the Dispensary, a faint illumination glowed from the walls, enough to see by. Cassidy ran her hand along the wall. Was this the accumulation of so many particles of dream dust? She stopped when she got to one of the framed artist's renderings of the Dreamkeeper as a comic book character. She touched the red coat's stained cuff with her fingertips, wondering if the two were related.

Paul, having parked the ship, leapt in behind them. He strode to a small cupboard she hadn't noticed by the window, pulled out a handgun, and checked for bullets. "The Dreamkeeper always kept it loaded in case the dreamless attacked," he told Cassidy when he caught her watching.

They entered the dispensary proper, Paul and Esmerelda stuffing bottles of dream dust into cloth sacks while Merrick slipped from the room, returning to the landing platform.

"Where are you going?" Cassidy asked him.

She didn't like his guilty expression. "I need to check on Aislyn."

"Aislyn?"

"The Dreamkeeper's wife, the woman who smuggled the dream dust out to Minseo. I'm worried he's done something terrible to her."

Cassidy glanced through the door he'd opened into the Dreamkeeper's house. It hadn't been locked. She lifted her arms and pulled her hair back into a snug ponytail. "I don't like that he left the door unlocked, Merrick." *Especially after leaving the coat to lure me here.* "I'll go instead; I've dealt with this sort of thing before and I'm already on his hit list. You help Ez and Paul gather the dust. You need to save your people."

For a moment she thought he was going to argue with her, but he didn't. Instead, he nodded and turned back the way he'd come.

Cassidy stepped over the threshold of the house and crept down a poorly lit hallway. Lights were on at random inside; the man was likely home. Comic panels, more elaborate than the ones hanging in the Dispensary, lined the walls. Together they displayed multiple pages of the same story, involving the Dreamkeeper and a woman called the Heroine Avenger. Although he was clearly the villain, the other was a hero. The woman had dark, flowing hair, her coveralls more than realistically provocative as she blended in with the citizens, seducing the Dreamkeeper for access to dream dust but falling in love along the way. Cassidy paused, piecing together reality versus the story depicted. Was the Heroine Avenger also Aislyn?

The Dreamkeeper was the same caricatured villain Cassidy had met that first day in the Dispensary, but the comic revealed that he, too, fell in love with his rival in a complicated dance of role play and burning sexual tension. The writer played with the concept of balance between good and evil, personified between the two.

In the climax panel, the Heroine Avenger revealed her name: Aislyn, while the Dreamkeeper refuses to acknowledge he has a name to put to his title. His lover is hurt and angry, breaking him down until he confesses that he abandoned his birth name when his parents sold him to the factories for a handful of dream dust. Small children came in handy for darting between moving gears. His only solace was his art, a nobody child scribbling pictures onto cobblestones between shifts. One day another boy stole his chalk. The Dreamkeeper beat the boy badly for it, his ruthlessness catching the eye of Bezanson who gave him both the title of Dreamkeeper and the chance to keep his imagination, and thus his art, indefinitely.

The story panels had led Cassidy into a wrecked studio. The smell of paint and ink hung thick, papers scattered, each of them a sketch of the Heroine Avenger with the Dreamkeeper, speech bubbles drawn but left empty. Cassidy crouched to pick one of the papers up, noticing the wedding rings and the initials DK in the corner.

"We are all of us a little disappointed in reality, aren't we?" asked the Dreamkeeper, revealing his location on the floor, dishevelled, an open flask in his hand. "That's why we like our dreams. After all, if you could recreate yourself into everything you ever wanted to be—more powerful, more invincible—why wouldn't you?"

Cassidy frowned at the Dreamkeeper in the picture she held. "But you're not just the villain, are you? You're also the artist and the husband."

He didn't answer right away, gazing drearily ahead. "I've lost my partner. She's the one that comes up with our stories. She's the one who figures out our story when it's broken. I'm lost without her."

Cassidy tried to piece together Aislyn's character. "How did she manage to keep her imagination into adulthood?"

"She had no family, nobody watching out for her when she was a kid. Rather than turning her imagination in for security when she came of age, she became the Heroine Avenger, evading Compliance Officers by dint of skill and a street kid's knowledge of the city's secrets."

Cassidy clenched her jaw. The cephalopods had sat by a wormhole and waited while the hero they needed was there all along. She frowned at the woman's picture. Someone who clearly wanted to be a hero, at that.

The Dreamkeeper struggled, drunkenly, to his feet. "That's my coat you're wearing."

Cassidy took it off and tossed it to him. He caught it with ease, she noticed. Not drunk then, or just accustomed to the disorientation. "The kid had nothing to do with it."

The Dreamkeeper checked his pockets, finding nothing. "Merrick? Oh, I doubt that. Aislyn told me all about him and his adorable HQ."

Cassidy held up the drawing. "This is you and her, I take it?"

"It is." His face filled with sorrow. "We were a dream team. We plotted everything: her daring escapes, my foils. A game of careful balance under the eyes of our unseeing CEOs."

Cassidy struggled to grasp his worldview. "Did the two of you really consider yourselves hero and villain?"

The Dreamkeeper sneered at her. "The nature of our relationship is none of your business. We were two halves of a whole, the opposite sides to the same coin."

"You knew she was stealing dust."

"Of course. We respected each other's work. She didn't steal more than I could cover for, and the chemist kid was never going to figure out the formula, anyway."

"So what? Did you guys get off on being each other's nemesis?" She tried not to make a face.

His expression turned sad, his mouth down-turned, his gaze falling to the pictures on the floor. "No. I was her true love, not her nemesis."

Cassidy arched an eyebrow. "You're not the reason she's missing?"

The Dreamkeeper shook his head and took a swig from his flask. "It was Bezanson, after all. A cruel stroke, don't you think? The symbolic father betrayed me worse than my real father."

Cassidy let the sketch in her hand flutter to the floor. "What did Bezanson do to her?"

Tears streamed freely down his cheeks. "He found out what she was doing. She got overly confident and tried to break into one of his bigger warehouses, where he caught her."

"Is she alive?" Cassidy wasn't sure she wanted to know.

The Dreamkeeper sighed, pressing a trembling hand to the crease between his brows. "He imprisoned her and ripped out her imagination." He kicked at the sketches scattered over the floor. "Our creative dream has ended, our partnership destroyed. No more stories, no more adventures, and no more Heroine Avenger."

"No, you've still got a chance. There's a virus infecting the citizens that's restoring their imaginations."

The Dreamkeeper threw back his head and laughed, a gob of spittle flying from his mouth. "Nice one. But even if it was true, Bezanson would never let anyone keep their imagination." He straightened his coat sleeves and buttoned the front of his scarlet coat, sliding his fingers into his pockets again as his jaw tightened. His arm relaxed, his right hand falling into his trouser pocket where he pulled out a loaded dream pistol and pressed against Cassidy's temple. "But I will be the Dreamkeeper she wrote me to be forever, and you have something that belongs to me."

Cassidy heard a scuffle of papers from behind her and silently cursed Merrick for following her. She reached into her pocket and pulled out the wedding ring she'd found inside the Dreamkeeper's coat as the Dreamkeeper cocked the pistol's trigger. She offered him the ring. "It's not too late, you can have everything back: Aislyn, the stories, the roleplay, everything."

"She made a better heroine than you," he said, snatching the ring. "She would have convinced me." He ground the barrel into Cassidy's temple, the cold metal warming from her body temperature. "Did they tell you what happens if you get a dream dose when you already have an imagination? Because I know you have one, it's the only way you could have gotten this far." He crept in close to whisper into her ear. "They say there's no more painful way to die." Cassidy closed her eyes.

A shot rang out, but it was the Dreamkeeper's body that slumped to the floor, not hers. The wedding ring skittered out of his hand and rolled out of his reach. Cassidy looked up in time to see Merrick lean against the doorframe at the far end of the studio, his eyes locked in horror on the ever-widening pool of blood spilling from the Dreamkeeper's head.

Cassidy ran to Merrick, flinging the gun from his hand. "You saved me, Mer, you really did."

He nodded, swallowing hard, pushing through the shock. "I killed someone, Cass." He winced. "I killed my friend's husband."

"You saved a lot of people today." She pulled him to his feet. "Come on, Merrick. There's more we have to save, focus on them."

He glanced back at the body, guilt oozing from his every movement.

CHAPTER FIFTEEN

If Paul and Esmerelda noticed Merrick's unusual quiet on the flight back to Nightfall, they said nothing. He stared ahead, unseeing, while Cassidy tried to give him space. Dammit. This was exactly what she didn't want to happen to him.

The sun peeked up over a bruised morning, lines of grey feathering the horizon. The sunrise should have felt like a brave new dawn with the Dreamkeeper gone, but instead something ominous hung in the air. Cassidy wondered if a person ever got used to watching the sun come up on an alien world.

A large crowd had gathered at the base of Nightfall and Paul landed the ship a few storeys up. When Cassidy stepped outside of the ship, she could see Minseo dispensing dream dust below. The chemist smiled cheerily and waved when she saw them. It troubled Cassidy that Aislyn had told the Dreamkeeper about Minseo and Merrick's work with the rebellion.

Esmerelda hauled a large sack of Dispensary dust onto her back, bottles tinkling, and she made her way to the crowd with Paul and Merrick beside her, clutching small sacks of their own. The light returned to Merrick's eyes when he saw the people waiting for their cure.

Cassidy hung back, unable to shake the feeling that something wasn't right. The factories sat quiet, everyone amassing here instead of work, but a steady burr echoed off the buildings. She climbed high up the side of Nightfall to get a better view.

A cephalopod hung nearby. It opened its eyes and watched her as she waved in greeting. She wished she knew if it was the same ceph she had spoken with, but it was dark then and her perspective from the ground was wildly different.

By the fifteenth floor, the burr clarified into the sound of an engine. She turned towards it, not surprised to see a larger airship flanked by two of the same black ships she had flown in moments ago. Cassidy hesitated, looking down at the crowd, their laughter and cheer rising into the morning cephalo-fog on the breeze. Maybe the ships were friendly.

Cassidy waited as the ships got closer. The airship had something large and rectangular strapped to its belly. She squinted to make out the details. It looked familiar. An IED, she realized, her heart sinking. She glanced down again, loathe to end the citizens' newfound joy. She turned to the cephalopod, whose eyes were open wide now, watching the ship come in. Cassidy crouched into the building below what might have been an air conditioning if she were back on Earth. Maybe if there was only a few Officers she could stop them or bribe them with the promise of their own imagination.

The airship appeared ready to pass over Nightfall, but slowed when the crowd in the broken square came into view. The smaller ships circled around while the airship landed on Nightfall, the building rumbling as the weight of the new IED settled onto the brick, its pilot clumsier than Paul and struggling with the angle. The two small ships landed softly at its side.

The laughter of the citizens below died as they noticed the new IED. For a long moment there was silence until it erupted into angry yells. Cassidy smiled, glad to hear them fighting back.

A man leaned over the edge of the airship's gondola. Bezanson himself. Cassidy recognized him from the film at Merrick's extraction. The man sneered at the crowd and signalled for his team to exit the small ships. Four soldiers trooped out of each, large guns in hand. "Kill as many as you need to frighten them into submission again," Bezanson ordered.

Cassidy's adrenaline spiked, sending her to her feet and leaping over windows and stacks as she ran toward the cephalopod. "You need to help them right now!" she shouted, willing the creature to understand her.

The cephalopod's eyes opened wide, its tentacles swimming through the air like water, moving faster than Cassidy could ever have expected, and positioned the considerable bulk of its body between Bezanson's goons and the citizens of Factorytown.

"Shoot the damn thing!" hollered Bezanson, his voice vibrating with rage.

The soldiers looked back at him, clearly shocked. When they met each other's eyes, their postures relaxed, their weapons clattering to the ground. Bezanson stomped his foot and stormed from the gondola to the side of the Nightfall. He grabbed one of the guns with a sneer on his face and spat bullets from the weapon into the cephalopod's eye.

Cassidy froze, the creature's ruined eye splashing down upon Bezanson and his goons. The cephalopod screamed, a vibrating, high-pitched squeal Cassidy felt in the bottom of her stomach. The creature emitted a cloud of red fog so dense that Cassidy could not see her hands in front of her. She crouched, looking around at the odd red cloud that smelled sharp and pungent, like a vinegar. *This is a distress signal*, she marvelled. Bezanson shouted in frustration further inside the cloud, Nightfall too dangerous to navigate without sight or foreknowledge.

When at last the fog dissipated, some two dozen cephalopods circled their wounded friend and Bezanson. Some coiled comforting tentacles around their friend, while another reached for the IED, rolling it up in its tentacles and squeezing, small parts crushing out and pinging as they fell against Nightfall.

A small cheer rose from the crowd below. Bezanson's soldiers abandoned him, heading for the ground as the remaining cephalopods crowded in around the CEO. Her view blocked, Cassidy followed the soldiers. Bezanson had sealed his own fate. She flinched at the garbled sounds he made as he met his end.

The soldiers held up their hands as they approached the citizens. "Is it true the dust restores your imaginations?" one of them asked.

Merrick grinned and clapped the speaker on the back,

offering him a dose.

"The CEOs are getting reports like this from all over. First everyone gets sick and then something happens to the dust," said another soldier.

Cassidy smiled to herself, looking back at the cephalopods gathered above. These people would be okay. It was time to go back to her own world. She smiled, turning from the scene and heading in her own direction. Through an alley, up one last flight of stairs, and into a familiar warehouse. The broken IED loomed in the centre, its seat still cracked with all the lives it destroyed, the space still tinged with fear and pain. She lingered over it, wondering if there was anything Gamgee could salvage from it. Then again, she didn't want that thing anywhere near Earth.

"Were you going to leave without saying goodbye?" asked Merrick from the doorway, out of breath from running up the stairs to catch her.

Cassidy grinned. "Yes, as a matter of fact. Important things are happening; you should be there. You're going to be an excellent leader, Mer, and the cephalopods want to help, but you're going to need to tell them when and how to do so," she said. "You'll be fine."

"Not if I don't watch out for my friends, I won't be," he countered. "Come on, let me help you. What do you have to do, jump out the window?"

Cassidy sighed, fishing around in the palette and pulling out her abaya. She flourished it in the air and pulled it over head, letting the cloth drape over her everything.

"What is that? Some sort of shroud?"

She laughed despite herself. "Not exactly."

"You never told me what happened to Aislyn."

Cassidy sighed, wishing she could lie and say the woman was dead. "The Dreamkeeper said she's still alive. Bezanson caught her breaking into a warehouse, extracted her imagination, and put her in prison."

"She had an imagination?" He shook his head. "She never said anything about that."

"Aislyn was a complicated woman. I wouldn't go looking for her, Mer. I know it's hard to understand, but the Dreamkeeper and Aislyn did love each other. She might not be happy to see you, considering, and I'm not convinced she's entirely stable."

His brow creased. She reached over and squeezed his hand. "You okay?"

He nodded. "I will be, we all will be, thanks to you."

"No, thanks to you, and to the cephs." She reached for a long coil of rope, tying one end to a metal pole and tossing the other out the window. "All right, friend, can you pull this up after you can feel my weight is off of it and promise me you'll never go down there?"

"You still haven't said goodbye," he told her.

"Listen, Mer. I'm not going to. Okay?"

He nodded, his eyes soft. She held his gaze for a long moment, before tucking through the window and out of his world.

Cassidy felt a wave of dry heat coming through that let her know the portal was close. A moment later, she slipped inside the strange inbetween space again. A cephalopod waited, staring, as ominous as they had been in the beginning. After a long pause, her lungs heavy with holding her breath, it spoke into her mind. "Thank you."

Then she was home. Well, Saudi Arabia, all dry heat

and daytime this time around. Cassidy struggled as the rope got caught up in her abaya, falling the last meter to the ground and slipping out of the lengthy fabric as she did so. Merrick immediately pulled the rope back up again, her abaya attached. "No wait!" But he couldn't hear her.

"Crud," Cassidy cursed, her head bare, her covvies still on. Digging through her pockets, she found the old kerchief near the bottle of dream dust and tied it over her hair. It was better than nothing. Reaching for her phone, she crouched against the barrel and called Gamgee. "I'm going to need an abaya and a rescue ASAP."

Gamgee sighed. "Cassidy."

"Hey, on the bright side I can speak every language in the universe now. That's got to be worth something, right?"

ACKNOWLEDGEMENTS

The authors would like to pay special thanks to the *Slipstreamers* committee at Engen Books, including Amanda Labonté, Matthew LeDrew, AJ Ryan, Ellen Curtis, Erin Vance, and, Lauralana Dunne.

Without their tireless efforts, none of this would have been possible.

Special thanks to this episode's editor, Ali House.

Jennifer Shelby would also like to thank Dorothy Hall for sharing her impressions of and experiences in Saudi Arabia. Peter J. Foote for believing in this story, offering advice, and fielding countless panicked messages when I wrote myself into a corner. And Mike O'Reilly, without whom my writing would not be possible.

COMING SOON!
QUEST FOR THE DIGITAL HEART
BY JD RYOT & JON DOBBIN!

The next incredible episode of Slipstreamers, Cassidy Cane and the Quest for the Digital Heart, will be available soon, written with bestselling author Jon Dobbin!

Cassidy ventures to a strange new world of advanced technology where one artifact -- the Digital Heart -- promises total control over the world's technology! Can she secure it before it's too late?

SPECIAL BONUS STORIES!

We're pleased to present four additional stories from this episode's incredible co-author, Jennifer Shelby.

Jennifer Shelby was born in Halifax, Nova Scotia and currently resides in Hopewell Hill, New Brunswick.

She is the author of many works of short fiction, including 'Mrs. Coleman's Backyard Refugee Camp' for *Andromeda Spaceways*, and 'Toby's Alicorn Adventure' for *Cricket*. She was featured in the 2020 anthology *Pulp Science-Fiction from the Rock*.

She brings with her: *Borrowed Wings*, originally published in the April 2016 issue of Spaceports and Spidersilks, *Mrs. Coleman's Backyard Refugee Camp*, originally published in the Issue 68 of Andromeda Spaceways, *Dragon Crossing*, originally published in the December 2018 issue of All Worlds Wayfarer, and the original story *Mr. Polyphemus*.

BORROWED WINGS

Darina discovered the wings of a luna moth in a scattered pile of leaf litter. At first she thought they must be the wings of some poor, dismembered fairy. After some research she knew better, but she couldn't shake the feeling they were connected, somehow, to the Wee Folk.

That summer Darina found wings everywhere. There were butterfly wings in parking lots, in ditches, and along the streets where she rode her bike; each one a grim memorial to a fragile being embedded in a grill or smeared across a windshield. She tucked them into paperbacks and pedalled them home, safe inside their literary sarcophagi.

She captured her collection within the sticky pages of an old-fashioned photo album. She labelled them with slips of paper, recording the date, the place she found them, and each wing's Latin name. She kept the pages on a bookshelf that sat above her bed and showed them to no one. They became Darina's dark and special secret.

One night in autumn she awoke to a flurry of half-broken fairies ransacking her bedroom. They wailed as they searched frantically for her collection of wings. Darina calmed the fairies with soft words and a lullaby. She bade them hold still while she worked with a bottle of glue, a sewing needle, and a thread of spider silk. One by one the fairies flitted off into the darkness, whole again on borrowed wings.

DRAGON CROSSING

First came the spooky feeling on his heels, a warning gust of wind in the trees. A shadow, half-seen, and a piteous moan. A monstrous, disembodied arm reached out to him. With a shriek, Gavin turned and ran, the gloss of the tombstones flashing in the moonlight.

Willow trees billowed up from the ground. Statues looked on in ominous silence across the cemetery's pond. He whirled around, looking for somewhere to hide.

"Graveyard's closed," said a raspy, female voice.

Gavin looked up, surprised. People usually took in his hairless head, his gaunt frame, and hospital gown and left him alone.

"State your business, please." A short, elderly woman, her skin a labyrinth of wrinkles, sat on a faux stone bench beneath a weeping willow. She wore a black patch over her left eye and a white braid hung over her shoulder. The knife in her hand caught the moonlight with a menacing glint.

"I was trying to get away from ..." Gavin glanced back. "From ..."

"Well, it must've been bad if it chased you into the

graveyard," quipped the woman. She sliced into a round fruit with her knife. "Pomegranate?"

He shook his head. "No, thank you."

She nodded, popped a few seeds into her mouth, and crunched them down. "I'm Morgan Whitmore, but folks call me Jinx. I'm the groundskeeper here."

"I'm Gavin." He tried not to stare at her eyepatch. "Do you work all night, alone, in a graveyard?"

Jinx shrugged. "I don't sleep well on the full moon."

"You live in the graveyard?"

"Sure. Little cottage at the edge of the property. Gives the added benefit of built-in security."

"Security from what? Ghosts?"

Jinx eyed him up and down. "From folks like you, I suppose. You get all sorts in graveyards."

Gavin remembered a joke his father used to tell him whenever they'd pass a cemetery. Used to. He'd stopped when Gavin was diagnosed with cancer. What was it again? Ah yes. *People are dying to get in there.* He peered at Jinx's shadowy face, wondering if she would appreciate the joke. He decided against it.

The monster moaned again, somewhere in the shadows. Gavin moved closer to the groundskeeper.

She squinted across the moonlit pond with her good eye and spat on the ground. "Sounds like someone's in agony."

The sound grew closer. Gavin wondered if he should run, but then he'd be alone. In a graveyard. At night. The willow trees and the pond were pleasant enough with the cheery full moon shining down, but it was still a cemetery.

A mist gathered atop the pond and a dark, unfocussed head materialized, dissolved, and materialized again. Jinx hissed, but she kept her seat.

What made her so brave? He stared up at the beast, a prickle of cold sweat on the back of his neck. It shifted, closer, the head appearing above him. For a moment, it looked familiar. He hesitated. A great gob of drool fell from the beast's jowls and slapped onto his face, slimy and stinking. Gavin retched and rolled off the bench, away from the horrible creature.

"Come on, we have to run!" Gavin grabbed Jinx's hand and tugged.

"We do?" She abandoned her snack and hobbled alongside him.

Past the willow grove and into a shadowy forest of tombstones they ran. Gavin led her behind a statue of an angel to catch their breath and wait.

The graveyard looked endless. *How many people do you think are dead in there?* Gavin heard his father ask, deep in some old memory. *All of them!*

Jinx peered back the way they'd come. "Is that your monster, then? This some sort of game?"

"What? I don't have a monster."

"You don't? You sure about that? Some folks get monsters without realizing it."

Gavin scratched his head and felt a shock of hair. He tugged at it, feeling it pull at his scalp. The hair was his.

"What are you yanking at your hair for? Are you some sort of crazy person?" asked Jinx.

"No. I just – I don't have hair."

Jinx looked him up and down. "You said you don't

have a monster, either, kid. Pardon me if I don't believe you."

Gavin discovered he wore a t-shirt and a pair of black pants. Not a hospital gown or pajamas. When had he changed clothes? He couldn't remember much before the monster.

"A monster's nothing to be ashamed of. I see strange things in my line of work. Not all of them with my good eye, either." She pointed at her eyepatch with her finger.

The ragged black fabric fascinated Gavin. "What's behind it?" He clapped his hand over his mouth, embarrassed he'd said it aloud.

The old woman threw back her head and cackled at the stars. "The cheek of it! Well, you're young after all, I suppose. But it's frightening, boy. Something like that," she said, "you can't unsee. You'll scream and run away."

"I won't," Gavin said. "I'm brave. I fought cancer."

She squinted at him. "Did you win?"

He couldn't remember, he realized. Strange. "I won't scream or run away. I promise."

Jinx sized him up a moment before lifting the eye patch and leaning towards him.

At first Gavin thought the skin had torn away with the fabric, but there was no skin. Just bone. The eye socket of a skeleton. And in that socket a wolf spider had spun its web. It stared back at him from its macabre cave, its front legs poised to pounce.

Gavin swallowed a scream, remembering his promise. He shoved his fear aside, the way he'd learned to do through endless surgeries. "What do you feed it?"

Jinx laughed, a dark, wheezy sound. "You don't want

to know. I like you, kid. I guess I'll help you out with your monster."

"I keep telling you, I don't have a monster."

Jinx leaned against the weeping statue. "You're what, eleven? Twelve? How long have you been sick?"

"Six years."

"So, you've been sick since you were five or so. In and out of hospitals, no doubt. Sleeping in scary places full of weeping parents and dying children. Chemotherapy. The pukes and the shakes. The cold that gets in your bones. You mean to tell me you never imagined yourself a friend to help you escape all that?"

He couldn't imagine why it mattered so much, but he told her. "I had a dragon named Zamfir."

Jinx screwed up her face like a withered apple. "You named your dragon after a pan flute player from the eighties? How old were you then, negative thirty?"

Gavin blushed. "They play a lot of old music in doctor's offices. Besides, Zamfir isn't a monster. He has scales like emeralds, eyes of amber, and he breathes a cobalt flame when I ask him to."

"So, ask him."

Fine. He'd prove her wrong. The audacity of thinking Zamfir a monster. "Hey, you!" Gavin shouted across the graves. "If you're Zamfir, breathe blue flames for me!"

A now-familiar mist collected beside the bereft angel. A bit of black scale came into focus. There, thought Gavin, Zamfir is green.

A popping sound followed by a rush of blue flame filled the air above him.

Gavin stared up, his jaw slack. "Zam?"

Jinx smacked her gums. "Crossing over's tough when you're imaginary. Still, he's luckier than some. You didn't grow up and abandon him."

"Crossing over?" Gavin looked down at his regular clothes, at the dim tombs surrounding him, at the smudge of blurry dragon hanging in the air. "Am I dead?" He tugged at his hair again. He didn't feel dead.

"I should say so!" Jinx hopped onto ancient tombstone and picked at her nose with a long fingernail.

Zamfir moaned. Gavin recognized it now. The sound of a dragon in mourning. He'd imagined this when he thought of what his funeral might be like.

"You're taking this rather well," said Jinx.

Being dead didn't hurt like living did. It didn't hurt at all. It felt good. Free. Strangely alive, somehow. "It's about time," he said, astonishing himself.

Jinx wiped her nail on her pants. "Best attitude to have, considering."

Gavin remembered his mother. His father. His brother and his baby sister. They must be so sad.

"Don't you go finding reasons to feel bad, now. We've got a dragon to save," said Jinx.

"We do?"

"Well, can't have him stuck between worlds. Piteous moans aren't good for my graveyard's reputation. I can get you started, but it's a tough job. Bright side is, if it works, you've got yourself a proper dragon for life. Well, death. Same difference. But you can't stay here. This is my graveyard. Deal?"

Gavin couldn't imagine why he would want to stay in the cemetery. "Deal."

Jinx jumped down from the tombstone and waddled towards a grove of maple trees.

"Where are we going?" asked Gavin.

"Mausoleum."

Gavin hesitated. People stored bodies in mausoleums. Dead bodies. His first instinct was to turn back, but he remembered he was dead himself. Strange, knowing that. Was this how healthy people felt every day? Strong limbs, settled stomach, breath coming easy, heart keeping time, and a stockpile of energy to spare? He wished Zamfir were here, they could play a wicked game of hide and seek in this place.

Behind him a piece of the unformed dragon whimpered.

"Sorry, Zam. I'd forgotten."

"Are you talking to yourself or to your imaginary friend?" demanded Jinx.

"Is there a difference?"

Jinx cackled. "There might be."

Before them loomed a stone wall built into the side of a hill. On the iron gate the name "Whitmore" wove into the design. Jinx's last name. Gavin tried not to think about what that might mean.

Jinx pulled a set of skeleton keys from her pocket and wiggled one into the lock. With a grunt she yanked off the padlock and the gate creaked open.

"You got any coins on you?" she asked.

Gavin dug into his pockets. To his surprise, he discovered two gold pieces.

Jinx nodded. "I thought so. Dead children often find an extra coin in case their parents decide to follow. They're meant for the boatman, so don't be giving them to anyone else or you'll be stuck worse than dear old dragon."

"What boatman am I supposed to pay?"

"Bah! Kids these days. Don't they teach you anything in school?"

Gavin blushed. He'd never been a good student.

"Well, you'll figure it out." Jinx stooped to a small, cupboard-sized door and opened it.

Gavin's mouth went dry. With a flicker of panic, he realized the hole wasn't the size of a cupboard. It was the size of a coffin. He shook his head. "I can't go in there."

Her mouth flattened into a grim line. "It's the only way to the other side." She crossed her arms. "Elsewise we'll have to be getting rid of your dragon the old-fashioned way."

"What does that mean?"

Jinx grinned, dark and toothless. Gavin followed her gaze to the edge of the crypt. Shadows gathered, growing darker, taking form. A beast with slathering jaws and eyes of living flame emerged in the gloom. Its snout grew and it sniffed at the air.

Gavin stepped back, the scent of sulphur burning in his nostrils. He must be dead, elsewise he would have soiled himself. "I'll go," he said, climbing inside the coffin cupboard.

Jinx reached past him and flicked on a light switch. The crypt filled with light. "Mind the ladder now."

The ladder rungs were slick with slime and pitted with rust. He stepped on the finger bones of a skeleton still gripping the ladder below him. The bones fell to the crypt floor with a crash and a puff of dust. The sound of his breath echoed in Gavin's mind, the taste of the dust on his lips. He stopped, gripping the ladder, waiting for his heart to steady. It had never beat so fast when he was alive.

"Follow the tunnel till you come to the river. I expect you'll find the rest of your dragon in there, swimming around with the other lost souls."

"You're not coming with me?" Gavin squeezed his eyes tight, hoping for a positive answer.

Jinx guffawed. "Me? Go in there? Can't do it, kid. I'm on the clock, remember? Graveyard shift. But you'll be all right. You got your coins. Have you remembered to bring your courage?"

"Sure. It's in my other pocket," Gavin said.

Jinx snickered and peered down at him. "Snarky. I like that. You're a good kid, Gavin. Best of luck with your dragon, and remember, you promised you'd leave in the end."

Gavin didn't answer. Some ally she'd proved to be.

"Keep those coins safe!" Jinx called into the gloom.

Gavin heard the door shut as he stepped off the ladder, giving the bones a wide berth. A row of bare lightbulbs above him fizzled and hissed, revealing a long, winding brick tunnel lined with coffins. He gulped, trying not to picture moldering corpses coming to life within them.

What did the casket say to the other casket? he remembered his dad asking. *That you coffin?*

He hurried down the tunnel. He wondered what his own casket was like. If his body was rotting yet. He clenched his fists. They were solid, whole, warm. This body felt real enough and it wasn't weak, it wasn't diseased, and it wasn't forever dying. This was his body now, he decided.

As he moved deeper, the bricks gave way to seeping rock walls. Stalactites formed in the warm damp, reaching down at him with stabbing fingers.

The lights flickered on and off. He found himself in darkness, reaching for the lights ahead. A massive cobweb stuck to his face as he stepped through it. He pulled the webbing from his face with a grimace, wondering if he'd somehow stumbled into Jinx's eye.

The steady drip of moisture grew thick, its plop heavier. Gavin tried not to think of blood as a warm splotch dribbled through his hair.

He heard a flutter of sound behind him, a squeak. Mice, or bats, he told himself. Footsteps shuffled, far behind him. He didn't dare look, afraid to turn and see Jinx's eye spider waving its legs at him.

An echo of chilling howls grew steadily louder. Too frightened to breathe, Gavin moved on through the shadows. A smudge of gray river flickered in the darkness.

He squinted at the river, his body tense. A myriad of human forms writhed and tumbled over each other in the mist. Theirs were the howls he'd heard.

Zamfir was in there, somewhere, all because of Gavin. He should have imagined the dragon capable of crossing over whenever he wanted. Gavin couldn't leave him there.

A path lined with jagged rocks and broken stalactites led Gavin to the riverbank. The river rose like a wall of thick mist. Ghostly, human shapes swirled in the current, reaching out to nothing, mouths open. The howling, Gavin realized, was the collective moaning and wailing of these …what were they? Ghosts? Wraiths? He gulped. Souls?

Gavin squinted into the grey smudge of river, looking for his dragon.

He paused, gathering his courage. It couldn't be worse than having cancer. Or dying.

Gavin closed his eyes and stepped into the current. It swept past him, more wind than water, tugging out his clothes as his ears filled with the moaning of the trapped dead. The chill of the river sank into his bones.

The wraiths turned to look at him, beseeching at first, then angry, their mouths open, baring inhuman fangs.

"Zam!" he called. The rush of the current swept his words away, drowning them in the wails of a myriad ghosts.

Gavin's hands began to shake.

"Zamfir!" How was he ever to find his dragon in this endless river? How could Zamfir hear his yells amidst the endless wails?

"Think Gavin," He peered into the blurry distance. This was hard. He'd always just imagined the dragon before and he would appear. Was Zamfir still imaginary, or was he real on this side of life?

Gavin's head spun. Death complicated things.

Something tugged at his pants. He looked down to see a wraith digging into his pocket His coins! Gavin backed away, tripping over a broken stalactite. He would have fallen hard, but the current caught him and bounced him along before depositing him in a hollow.

The wraith smiled, its mouth spread into a ghastly grimace. A shine of gold flickered in its hand.

Gavin reached into his pocket. A single coin remained. A cold, dark feeling washed over him.

The gold attracted the attention of other wraiths. Within a moment, a crowd gathered, each of them ripping at his pants with clawed fingers. Some swiped at him with their teeth, anything to get his precious coin.

Jinx's warning echoed in his ears. If he lost the coin, he'd be stuck in this place forever, and so would Zamfir. Gavin kept fighting, curling his legs into his belly and gripping them to protect the coin as he grew tired.

Tears trickled down his face. He'd failed. He'd never last against this endless army of the lost dead. He'd lost his fight with cancer. He'd lost his dragon. And now he'd lose his last coin too.

The hands of the ghosts battered against him, but he ignored them, curled up in his little ball. Moments like these were not unfamiliar to a boy who fought cancer. These were the moments that birthed an imaginary dragon. What happened if he died a second death in a river of lost souls? Did he have to stay here forever?

He only had one coin left. He could save himself.

No. It would be better if he gave the coin to Zamfir. He'd imagined Zamfir as the cleverest dragon in seventy kingdoms. Zamfir would find a way back in here, and he'd save Gavin right back. He knew Zamfir wouldn't give up on him.

A sudden roar drowned out the snarling dead. Gavin lifted his head to see the ghost of a mighty dragon tossing the ghosts aside in a fury. "Zam!"

The dragon clutched Gavin to his chest and cooed, giving the boy a questioning look.

"I came to save you," Gavin explained. "I had these coins. This groundskeeper, Jinx, she told me we could use them to get out of this place, but then all the other ghosts tried to steal them and ..."

Zamfir nuzzled the top of his head with his nose, gurgling deep in his throat.

"We give them to some guy in a boat, and he'll take us out of here." It seemed ridiculous when he said it out loud. Why did he believe everything Jinx said, anyway? What did he know about her, besides the creepy spider in her eye socket?

The dragon nodded, his scaly brow furrowed in concern.

Gavin stopped. "It's good to see you again, Zam." He gave the dragon another hug. Through the moldy, earthy smell of the river, he could smell a whiff of new mown lawn and campfire. It was just the way Gavin always imagined his dragon would smell like.

Zamfir helped Gavin onto his back, giving the wraiths another warning growl.

"Have you seen anyone with a boat?" Gavin asked.

Zamfir gurgled, deep in his gullet. Gavin interpreted it as a maybe.

The dragon pushed off, drifting into the dark current. Gavin clutched at the beast's scales as wraiths swooped past, shrieking.

They travelled this way until the current pushed them close to the far edge of the river. Fluorescent lights and a rush of hospital foot traffic showed through the grey. Gavin watched in awe, had he just died? Hadn't he been here, on the other side, all night?

With a beat of his wings, Zamfir broke through the edge of the river, the pair of them sprawling on the hospital linoleum.

A nurse ran through them, carrying an IV bag into the children's oncology ward.

"We're ghosts now," Gavin realized.

Zamfir gurgled to the sky.

Gavin giggled. "Yeah, now I'm imaginary too." He got to his feet.

Waves lapped at the tiles beneath his feet. Shocked, Gavin turned around. Behind them a wide gray river yawned into a dark cave. A ghostly hand rose from the waves and sank below again. A boat, large enough for a boy and his dragon, moved steadily towards them, slicing through the waves with a pointed prow carved with the likeness of a dragon and marked with a series of unfamiliar runes.

Gavin clutched one of Zamfir's claws, trying to think of a way to get the dragon to board without him.

The boat slowed to a stop before them. Gavin took a deep breath. A shrouded figure held out a hand. "Pay me gold or make me laugh," he said in a gravelly voice.

Gavin exchanged looks with his dragon. "Make you laugh?" he asked.

The boatman waited, saying nothing.

He remembered one last joke from his father's endless repertoire. Gavin took a deep breath. "Why didn't the skeleton cross the river?"

The boatman held a bony finger to his lips. Gavin's hopes evaporated. He hadn't realized the boatman was a skeleton.

"Why?" asked the boatman.

Gavin squeezed Zamfir's claw. "Because he didn't have the guts!"

Gavin exchanged a worried glance with Zamfir. He wished he'd remembered more of his dad's jokes.

The boatman shook his head. Gavin's heart thudded in his ears as his hopes fell. "Here's your coin, Zam. You go first, I want to say goodbye to the hospital." He pressed the lonely gold coin into the dragon's paw and watched his friend board the boat.

The boatman held out his hand to Gavin. Gavin shook his head. "You shall not cross," said the boatman.

Zamfir screamed as the boat moved off shore.

"It's all right, Zam! You're clever! I imagined you cleverer than I am! You can come back and rescue me this time."

Zam tried to fly from the boat, but he couldn't. Gavin never imagined him stronger than Death. They disappeared into the darkness, the dragon's screams muffled in the distance. Tears streamed down Gavin's face. He closed his eyes, ready to return to the awfulness of that grey river.

Beep.

Beep.

Beep.

The familiar trill of the heart monitor comforted the boy. He missed his dragon. Everything hurt.

"Gavin? Gavin can you hear me?"

"Mom?" Gavin opened his eyes. The river hadn't swallowed him up. He was in the hospital, his mom and dad smiling down at him, looking frightened and relieved all at once. He closed his eyes, tears slipping from his eyelids. He'd lost Zamfir.

"Thought we'd lost you, bud," said his dad.

"Your heart stopped, honey. We were so scared." His mom dabbed at his tears with a soggy tissue.

"I lost my dragon," Gavin said. He couldn't think of anything else.

His mom and dad exchanged worried glances.

His dad tittered the way he did when he was nervous. "Hey, bud. What do you get when a dragon sneezes?"

"What?"

"Out of the way!"

Gavin tried to smile. "I need to remember that one."

"Glad you're still with us," added his dad.

"Yeah." He missed his hair. His body ached. It felt weak. He wondered how long it would take Zamfir to rescue him. "But I don't think I'll be here much longer, okay?"

His mother gasped. His dad nodded in silence.

"Yeah. We know."

"It's not so bad on the other side. It doesn't hurt. It felt great. I rescued my dragon and met this old woman who kept a spider in her eye socket."

He didn't like the way they were staring at him. "I'm sorry. I mean, I missed you, but it was okay. I was okay. And I remembered your jokes!"

His dad squeezed his hand.

"I love you guys." His eyelids were heavy. Too heavy to keep open.

The heart monitor screeched. His mom started to cry. His dad held his hand, steady and firm. Gavin could smell campfire and new mown lawn. Instead of his father's hand he felt a cold coin pressed into his hand. He smiled to himself. He knew Zamfir would save him.

MR. POLYPHEMUS

The moth fluttered against Levi's bedroom window. He knew it was a Polyphemus moth because he'd seen it there the night before, drinking in the moonlight. It intrigued him enough that he looked it up in one of his great-aunt's natural history books.

Old people had books like that, Levi noticed. All of his books were digital, but he liked the feel of pages turning, the sensation of hunting for information. His dad would have looked it up on some app if he was around. Great-aunt Eliza didn't have a smart phone. She ... no, *they* lived so far in the mountains cell phones got terrible reception.

They'd called her on a landline to give her the news of his family's demise, and she'd trundled out to get him in an ancient pickup truck more rust than metal.

Levi didn't know his life anymore. He didn't know his house, his bedroom, his school, or even his great-aunt. He wished he'd died with his family. Levi knew this was a terrible thing to wish, but his grief demanded it.

The moth fluttered again, a faint tapping of wings against the glass. Worried it might hurt itself, Levi opened the window. The moth flew in.

It settled on his desk, staring at Levi, or so he supposed. Its fuzzy, orange body loomed like a lion's mane around the moth's small face, from which erupted two long, feathered antennae. Tan wings stretched to ragged tips, slowly shifting up and down while owlish eyespots winked in the evening light.

"What are you doing here, Mr. Polyphemus?" Levi flicked on the desk lamp to get a better look at the moth. Light spilled off the desk, onto the floor. Shadows fled into their corners, whimpering. Levi paid them little heed.

One shadow reached out across the floor from underneath the dresser. It slithered along the floorboards, defying the physics of shadows. The farthest tendril of this shadow almost touched Levi's foot, but he sat down on the bed and drew his feet up at the last moment.

The Polyphemus moth shifted to face the shadow head on.

"What is it?" Levi asked.

The moth didn't answer. Moths don't talk.

Levi leaned forward, catching a glimpse of the shadow reaching out from beneath the dresser. He froze. Something about that shadow set his spine alive with shivers and thickened his blood with slush.

Levi leaned back, willing his eyes away from the thing. He fixed them on the moth instead, who now stood perched, wings up and ready to fly, antennae waving. It stepped forward to the extreme edge of the desk.

The shadow moved from beneath the dresser and oozed up the wall across from Levi. The light of the desk lamp had no effect upon this shadow. He watched with fascinated horror as it convulsed and shaped itself into his mother. She beckoned to Levi before morphing into his father, and finally into his little sister.

He blanched in the light of the desk lamp as their shadow ghosts writhed before him, cold, altered, and somehow not quite them.

The shadow turned into the car that shattered them to pieces and left Levi an orphan, living with his great-aunt and a landline and weird books about moths. It played out the scene before his eyes as his fists clenched at the quilt his great-aunt said she'd sewn by hand.

Levi caught his breath as the shadow took his own shape. The shape of a boy who wished he had died with his family. The shadow had come for him, he realized, come to grant his wish for death. Come to make him a shadow ghost like them.

For the first time, Levi felt afraid of dying.

He didn't want his body burnt up in a crematorium while his great-aunt wept over him. He wanted to live, even if he had to live a different life than the one he'd expected, the one he'd planned. He had an aunt with a heart good enough to take him in and offer him what love she had to give. He could try this life. It might not be so bad.

"I want to live," he said, his voice little more than a whisper.

The Polyphemus moth nodded once and leapt from the desk. Its wings fluttered fast enough to blur as it flew straight into the shadow of death.

The moth tangled the shadow in its tiny, barbed feet, drawing it further into the light. It began to shred the shadow, slow and methodical, between its feet. The shadow shriveled, writhing about the moth, but did little more than flick a bit of dust from its wings.

They twisted together in the air, the shadow growing smaller as the moth tore it into trifling fragments. The fragments wafted to the floor like ash and disappeared.

Levi watched with wonder as the moth finished up the last of the shadow and fell to the floor. The eyespots on its wings winked once and grew still.

Levi cupped the moth in his hands, unsure of why it saved him, why it came to help him, or how it knew.

For two days he left the Polyphemus moth atop his desk, hoping it would move or come to life again. He didn't know how to check a moth's pulse.

On the third day, great-aunt Eliza gave him an old jar to preserve it in. She confessed to him she'd kept butterflies this way when she was young.

Levi placed the moth inside with care and screwed on the lid. He kept it by his bed, and never failed to say "Goodnight, Mr. Polyphemus," before he shut the light and returned the room to shadows.

MRS. COLEMAN'S BACKYARD REFUGEE CAMP

BRRRRRRRRRRRRing!

Jackson put the phone to his ear.

"Jackson, it's your mother. Terrible news. You know that huge tract of enchanted forest where you and your sister used to play?"

Jackson chuckled at the memory. "Sure, we had so much fun playing there."

"They've chopped it down. All five hundred acres of it. Going to grow mustard or some such thing."

Jackson closed his eyes. He wished she hadn't told him. "Ah. Well. I guess we should have bought it ourselves if we wanted to keep it."

"Oh, don't be so stoic, it's terrible! All of those imaginary creatures have nowhere to go. They're roaming around the whole county, homeless! No one considers habitat loss anymore."

"Especially imaginary habitat loss."

"What?"

"If you're so worried about them, why not set up an imaginary refugee camp?" Jackson pictured his ma in her kitchen on the old, red rotary dial phone, surrounded by imaginary beasts. He chuckled, enjoying the game. "You have all that space in the backyard."

Silence.

"Ma?"

"That's a wonderful idea! I think I'll do just that."

Mrs. Coleman hung up.

Jackson put down the phone, regretting his suggestion. His mother had always had an overactive imagination. Sometimes he worried about her out there alone on the farm.

***

BRRRRRRRRRRRing!

"Jackson? It's me."

"Ma! It's three in the morning."

"I know, I'm sorry, I didn't know who else to call. I've got a troll! Are they dangerous?"

"A troll?" Jackson sat up, flinging his sleep mask across the room. Was she blogging again, after what happened last time? He couldn't afford to post bail again. "Don't panic, trolls are all the same. Just don't feed them."

Silence.

"Wow, Jackson. That's incredibly racist. I raised you better than that."

"Racist? What are you talking about? Everyone knows you can't acknowledge trolls. It only makes them worse."

"Hmmm. Well, the village is putting in a new bridge this summer. He could go there when it's finished. It seems terrible to feed everyone but him. I don't think I'm that kind of person."

"Ma, what are we talking about here?"

"Nothing, dear. Go back to sleep. I'm sorry I bothered you."

***

BRRRRRRRRRRRRing!

"Hello?"

"Jackson, it's me. Listen, I don't think you should bring the kids out this weekend."

Jackson never expected to hear those words from his mother. "Are you sure?"

"I am. The fairies have arrived. I guess they've just returned from some sort of pixie migration. They aren't sweet and dreamy at all. They're spoiled, temperamental little monsters. They put my hair in dreadlocks, Jackson. Dreadlocks! I'm seventy-two years old! I can't pull this off!"

Ah, so that's what this was about. Jackson took off his glasses and rubbed the bridge of his nose. "Ma, calm down. It's just a bad hairdo. The kids won't care."

"I'm not worried about them seeing my hair. Imagine what these little beasts might do to my beloved grandkids! They should be migrating again in a few weeks, and then it should be safe to come."

Jackson sighed. "Okay. We'll delay our visit."

"Oh, and Jackson? Could you mail me a box of fly swatters? They're all out in the village."

"Um … okay."

***

BRRRRRRRRRRRRing!

"Hello? Jackson?"

"It's me. What's up?"

"You remember my backyard refugee camp? Well, the septic's backed up. I guess it couldn't handle the extra ... well, you know. Plopsies. It's a real mess."

One of Jackson's eyelids started twitching. "If you're going to insist on having an imaginary refugee camp, shouldn't you at least imagine proper infrastructure?"

Mrs. Coleman's voice lowered to a whisper. "I didn't expect imaginary creatures would go this much! They never do in fairy stories. The unicorn has filled the whole stable! I'm too old to be mucking it out, and you know how my heart is -"

Jackson interrupted, exasperation in his voice. "Why don't you get the troll you were complaining about last week to do it?"

Silence.

"Ma?"

"That's an excellent idea! You always were smart. Do you remember when you won first place in the fifth grade science fair? You were so proud."

"Goodnight, Ma."

***

BRRRRRRRRRRRRing!

"Jackson?"

"Yes, Ma?"

"Do you know if veterinarians treat lake monsters?"

"Lake monsters?"

"Yes, she's been living in the pond, but it's rather small for her, and now's she got a cold from being over-exposed. Oh, it's awful. I'm afraid the whole place will collapse every time she sneezes."

Jackson drummed his fingers on his desk. He didn't have time for nonsense today. "Would you go to the doctor if you had a cold?"

Silence.

"I suppose you're right. Oh dear. Do you think everyone else is going to get it now? Imagine the dragon with a cold! I'd better order a pallet of tissues and a few fire extinguishers."

Jackson tugged at his hair. "Again, if you're going to imagine all of this, why not imagine everyone healthy?"

"Don't patronize me, Jackson. You have no idea how much work goes into a refugee camp."

Jackson stared in horror at a plug of hair he'd pulled from his head. Those plugs had cost a fortune. "Ma, be careful, okay? This is going a bit far. If you can't handle living out there by yourself, we're going to have to start thinking of other options. "

"Are you threatening to put me in a home, young man?"

Jackson shuddered. She'd used her spanking voice. "Calm down, Ma. I just want you to be careful."

"Goodbye, Jackson."

***

"Ma?"

"Oh, hello, Jackson! How are you, dear?"

"You haven't called in weeks, Ma. I got worried."

Mrs. Coleman giggled. "Oh, I'm fine, dear. I've started seeing someone and, well, you know what it's like at the beginning of a relationship."

"You're seeing someone? Who?"

"Don't get angry, your father's been gone for over a decade. I've been more than faithful to his memory. You remember the troll I told you about?"

"Yes." His voice sounded shrill.

"Well, I did feed him, after all, and now we're in love! Sure, I know he's green and rather ugly by human standards, but he's got such a sweet nature."

Jackson took a deep breath and grasped at the nearest straw. "Are you sure you should be getting into a relationship right now? I mean, you said running the camp was so much work."

"Oh, no, the camp is running fine now. I took your advice regarding the stable and used it all over. The ogres dug up the old septic tank and the dragon is incinerating the sewage from now on. I've even got the farm running again! Everyone puts in a few hours of labor a day. It keeps them busy and should make the camp self-sufficient by harvest. Unicorn manure is an amazing fertilizer, and you should see the minotaur plow a furrow! I might take him to the agricultural fair this year. Oh! I've got to go - the dragon is roasting marshmallows for everyone. Give the kiddos a kiss for me!"

ON SALE NOW FROM ENGEN BOOKS

When fifteen-year-old Phoenix loses her caregiver, everyone that she has ever known inexplicably turn their backs on her. Given the impossible burden of repaying an unknown debt, Phoenix sets out on her own with her trusty donkey, Muler, as her only companion. A chance encounter with Malcourt, a mysterious traveller, not only saves her life, but sets it on a trajectory that she would have never thought possible.

ABOUT THE AUTHOR

Jennifer Shelby hunts for stories in the beetled undergrowth of New Brunswick's fairy-infested forests. She fishes for them in the dark space between the stars. These stories, and many others, are made available through her catch-and-release program. You can learn more at jennifershelby.ca or on twitter @ jenniferdshelby.

Plague of the Dreamless: A Slipstreamers Adventure is her first novella.

JD Ryot is the reclusive creator of the *Slipstreamers* series from Engen Books. JD is an avid fan of young adult literature and adventure serials. When asked if they had come to this world through a portal themselves, JD Ryot refused to answer. No record of their birth has ever been found... on this world.